PROTECTING THE WIDOW

Roland looked up at her, his hands still fondling the dog. "You're not allowed to see anybody, what it is. I mean any man that might have serious or sexu'l intentions."

"I beg your pardon," Karen said.

"I'm supposed to keep 'em away from you. Any man believed to be serious—you know, not the grocery boy or something—I tell him to keep moving."

"That's what I was afraid of," Karen said. "I guess I'll have to have a talk with Mr. Grossi."

"Well, there's a little more to it."

"This is Ed Grossi's idea, isn't it?"

"No, it's your husband's idea."

"My husband's?"

"He left word, no man gets near you in a serious way or as a one-nighter just fooling around or anything like it as long as you live. In other words, your husband's cut off your action."

"Dashiell Hammett, Raymond Chandler,
John D. MacDonald.
The most recent is Elmore Leonard."
—*Washington Post Book World*

Bantam Books by Elmore Leonard
Ask your bookseller for the books you have missed

ESCAPE FROM FIVE SHADOWS
GOLD COAST
GUNSIGHTS
LAST STAND AT SABER RIVER
THE LAW AT RANDADO
THE SWITCH
VALDEZ IS COMING

GOLD COAST

ELMORE LEONARD

BANTAM BOOKS
TORONTO • NEW YORK • LONDON • SYDNEY • AUCKLAND

For Bill Leonard

GOLD COAST
A Bantam Book / December 1980
2nd printing ..... May 1985

ISBN 0-553-25006-X

Published simultaneously in the United States and Canada

Bantam Books are published by Bantam Books, Inc. Its trademark, consisting of the words "Bantam Books" and the portrayal of a rooster, is Registered in U.S. Patent and Trademark Office and in other countries. Marca Registrada. Bantam Books, Inc., 666 Fifth Avenue, New York, New York 10103.

PRINTED IN THE UNITED STATES OF AMERICA

H 11 10 9 8 7 6 5 4 3 2

1.

One day Karen DiCilia put a few observations together and realized her husband Frank was sleeping with a real estate woman in Boca.

Karen knew where they were doing it, too. In one of the condominiums Frank owned, part of Oceana Estates.

Every Friday afternoon and sometimes on Monday, Frank would put his spare clubs in the trunk of his Seville—supposedly to play at La Gorce, Miami Beach—and drive north out of Fort Lauderdale instead of south.

There were probably others, random affairs. Frank did go to Miami at least twice a week to "study the market" and play a little gin at the Palm Bay Club. He could have a cocktail waitress at Hialeah or Calder. He visited the dogtracks regularly, the jai-alai fronton once in awhile. Cruised for gamefish out in the stream with some of his buddies; went bonefishing in the Keys, near Islamorada, several times a year. Frank could have something going anywhere from Key West to West Palm, over to Bimini and back and probably did. The only one Karen was sure of, though, was the frosted-blonde thirty-six-year-old real estate woman in Boca.

Frank's actions, his routine, were predictable; but not his reactions. If she confronted him, or hinted around first, with questions like, "Do I know her?" or, "Are you going to tell me who she is?"

Frank would say, "Who're we talking about?"

And Karen would say, "I know you've got a girl friend. Why don't you admit it?"

And Frank would say—

He might say, "Nobody told you I have a girl friend and you haven't seen me with anybody that could be a girl friend, so what're we talking about?"

And Karen would say, "The real estate woman in Boca," and offer circumstantial evidence that wouldn't convict him but would certainly put him in a corner.

He might deny it out right. Or he might say, "Yeah, sometimes I go to Boca. Not that it's any of your fucking business."

Then what? She'd have to get mad or pout or act hurt.

So Karen didn't say a word about the real estate woman. Instead, she drove her matching white Caddy Seville up to Boca one Friday afternoon, to the big pink condominium that looked like a Venetian palace.

She located Frank's white Seville in the dim parking area beneath the building, on the ocean side, backed it out of the numbered space with the spare set of keys she'd brought, left Frank's car sitting in the aisle, got into her own car again and drove her white Seville into the side of his white Seville three times, smashing in both doors and the front fender of Frank's car, destroying her own car's grille and headlamps and drove back to Lauderdale. When Frank came home he looked from one matching Seville to the other. Karen waited, but he didn't say a word about the cars. The next day he had them towed away and new matching gray ones delivered.

Weeks later, in the living room, she said, "I'm getting tired of tennis." And said to the dog, sniffing around her feet, "Gretchen, leave, will you? Get out of here."

"Play golf," Frank said. He patted his leg and the gray and white schnauzer jumped up on his lap.

"I don't care for golf."

"Join some ladies' group." Gently stroking the schnauzer.

"I've done ladies' groups."

"Take up fishing, I'll get you a boat."

"Do you know what I do?" Karen said. "I exist. I sit in the sun. I try to think up work for Marta and for when the gardener comes—" She paused a moment. "When we got married—I mean at our wedding reception, you know what my mother said to me?"

"What?"

"She said, 'I hope you realize he's Italian.' She didn't know anything else, just your name."

"Half Italian," Frank said, "half Sicilian. There's a difference. Like Gretchen here"—stroking the dog on his lap, the dog dozing—"she's part schnauzer, part a little something else, so that makes her different."

"You don't get it, do you?" Karen said.

"Get what? She's from Grosse Pointe. I lived in Grosse Pointe one time. What's that? You buy a house."

"She wasn't being a snob. At least not when she said it."

"All right, what did she mean I'm Italian? What was she? Hill, maybe it was shortened from Hilkowski. Are you a Polack maybe? What're we talking about?"

"What she meant," Karen said, "the way you lived, what you were used to. You'd probably be set in your ways. You'd have your man things to do, and I'd have to find woman things to do. And she was right, not even knowing anything about what you really did, or might still be doing, I don't know, since you don't tell me anything."

"I'm retired," Frank said, "and you're tired of playing tennis and sitting around. All right, what do you want to do?"

"Maybe I'll just do it and not tell you," Karen said.

"Do what?" Frank asked.

"Not tell you where I go or who I see. Or make up something. Tell you I'm going to play tennis but I don't, I go someplace else."

"Stick to tennis," Frank said. He stopped stroking Gretchen. "You have a very hard time coming right out and saying something. You want to threaten me, is that it? Because you're bored? Are you telling me you're gonna start fooling around? If that's what you're saying, say it. A man comes to me and gives me some shit out the side of his mouth. I tell him that's it, get the fuck out or talk straight. Now I'm much more patient with you, Karen, you're my wife and I respect you. You're an intelligent, good-looking woman. I tell you something, I know you understand what I'm saying. I'm not dumb either, even though I didn't go to the University of Michigan when I was younger or one of those. Especially I'm not gonna *look* dumb, like have people point to me and say, 'Yeah, that's the guy, his wife's ballin' the tennis pro, the dumb fuck's paying the bill,' anything like that. No—you get bored and a little irritable, okay, use your head, work it out some way. But don't ever lie to me, all right? Or threaten me, like you're gonna pay me back for something. I know all about paying back. I could write a book about paying back then look at it and realize I left a few things out."

"My mother was right," Karen said. "You can do anything you want, but I can't."

"Your mother— You're a big girl," Frank said, "you were a big girl, what?, forty years old when we got married. You should know a few things by forty years old, uh, what it's gonna be like married to a half-Italian with varied and different business interests. You know what it's like? In the Bible. You got this house, eight hundred grand—sightseers come by the Intercoastal in the boats, look at it, 'Jesus Christ, imagine living in a place like that.' You got the apartment in Boca on the ocean. You got clothes, anything you want to buy. Servants, cars, clubs—"

"Go on," Karen said. "I have a dog—"

"Place in the Keys. Friends—"

"Your friends."

"I'm saying it's like in the Bible, you got anything you want to make you happy. Except there's one thing you're not allowed to do, and it's not even unreasonable, it's the natural law."

"What is?"

"A wife's faithful to her husband, subject to him. It's in the Bible."

"If I don't tell you what I'm doing, I'm being unfaithful?"

"What do you want to argue for? Haven't I been good to you? Jesus Christ, look around here, this place. The paintings, the furniture—"

"Your first wife's antiques."

"I don't get it. Five years, you don't say a word—"

"Five and a half," Karen said.

"Okay, there's some very rare, valuable pieces here. I happen to like this kind of stuff," Frank said. "But anything you don't like, sell it. Redecorate the whole place if you want."

"Keep me busy."

"What's the *matter* with you?"

Saying she was bored and irritable—while he went off to visit his girl friend in Boca, a real estate woman. Five and a half years of playing the good wife and now having the Bible thrown at her.

Karen made a mistake then, but was too angry to realize it at the time.

She gave Frank an ultimatum. She said, "No more double standard. If it's all right for you to fool around, it's all right for me to fool around. I may not want to, but I'll do it, buddy, as a matter of principle and you can see how you like it."

Frank seemed tired. He shook his head and said, "Karen, Karen, Karen—" and began stroking the dog again.

She did have misgivings later, twinges in her stomach whenever she thought about it and realized she had actually threatened him to his face. If that wasn't being a big girl, what was? She was relieved he never brought it up and would reassure herself with thoughts like, Of course not. Frank knew she'd never have an affair. Frank knew she had simply overstated, that was all, to make a point.

She would replay the scene in her mind and revise it

as she went along, keeping her voice in control, maintaining poise. Relying more on innuendo than outright threat. Hinting that she might fool around rather than throwing it in his face. She would recall later that the scene, the argument, had taken place May 10. A date to remember.

On December 2, the same year, Frank was admitted to Holy Cross Hospital with an oxygen mask pressed to his face, a rescue-unit fireman pounding on his chest. He died that afternoon in the Intensive Care Unit at age sixty-one.

Karen couldn't believe it. Forty-four years old and widowed for the second time, having outlived two Franks, one an automotive engineer, the other with "varied and different business interests." Aware of herself and feeling—how? analyzing it—feeling relief after the funeral and the mile-long procession with police escort to Memorial Gardens. Feeling—afraid to admit it at first—great. Free. More than that, excited. No more wondering after five years if she'd made a terrible mistake. Off the hook and looking forward to a new life.

Then discovering within the next few months that Frank DiCilia had as tight a hold on her dead as he did when he was alive.

She would look back. How did I get here? Trying to see a pattern, a motive.

Restless?

Karen Hill. A nice girl. Polite, obedient, a practicing Catholic. B-student through Dominican High and the University of Michigan, arts major. Accepted popular ideas about happiness along with a list of shoulds and shouldn'ts.

But, looking back, did she?

Yes, pretty much. Meet a nice guy with a future and get married, raise a family. The nice guy was Frank Stohler, Michigan '52. Neck a lot but don't go to bed with him until married: June, 1954, at St. Paul's On-the-Lake. Reception, Grosse Pointe Yacht Club. Finally to bed with big, considerate Frank Stohler who never made a sound or said a word making love. Rhythm method, no Pill yet. A daughter, Julie, born September, 1956.

The period with the first Frank was a lump of time. What did they do? Lived in two houses. Joined Lochmoor, the Detroit Athletic Club. Spent an annual business weekend at the Greenbriar. Went to Chrysler Corporation new-model show, SAE conventions. Restless. Was this her role? Played tennis, racquetball, paddleball, a little bridge, argued with Julie. Worried about her. Went to the theater or a dinner party every weekend. Refused to let Julie go to Los Angeles to study drama. She went anyway and was now appearing almost daily in *As the World Turns* and was good in a young bitchy part. What else?

Death. Her father and the first Frank within ten months of each other; both cardiac patients a short time and then gone. A little over two hundred thousand dollars in life insurance and Chrysler Corporation stock. Restless. A chance to do something else, be someone else. Sold the house in Grosse Pointe and moved to Lauderdale. Why? Why not? Got a job in real estate. Boring. Quit. And was introduced to Frank DiCilia at the Palm Bay Club.

The real and authentic Frank DiCilia out of Detroit newspaper stories about grand jury indictments and Organized Crime Strike-force Investigations, linked to perjury trials, the Teamsters, Hoffa's disappearance.

The widow and the widower, both eligible, both eyeing each other, but for different reasons.

She said to herself, This isn't you at all. Is it? Fascinated by the man and all the things he must know but never talked about. She liked his hands, even the diamond on the little finger. She liked his hair, still dark and thick, parted on the right side. She liked the dreamy expression in his eyes and the way he looked at her—Frank DiCilia looking at *her*—and she liked to look back at him calmly to show she wasn't afraid. Not feeling restless anymore. She could not imagine the first wispy-haired Frank with the second dark Frank. Engineers said they were engineers and drew cross-section pictures on paper napkins of how things worked. Frank and his associates never said what they were or wrote anything down. She asked Frank DiCilia directly, "What do you do?"

He said, "I'm retired."

She said, "From what?"

He said, "Industrial laundry business."

She said, "Are you in the Mafia?"

He said, "That's in the movies."

She visited his home in the Harbor Beach section of Lauderdale—her present address, 1 Isla Bahía—and said, "The laundry business must've been pretty good."

He said, "I'm in a little real estate, too."

She said, looking at the decor, the Sotheby estate-sale furnishings and Italian marble, "You could charge admission."

He said, "If you're not comfortable I'll sell it." But did not mention it again until May, five and a half years later.

She remembered another girl by the name of Hill, Virginia Hill, on television during the Kefauver investigations, the girl in the wide-brimmed hat and sunglasses who was the girl friend of a gangster. Karen had watched her, fascinated, wondering what it would be like.

That was part of it. Finding out. To walk with Frank DiCilia, aware of it; to enter La Gorce, Palm Bay, Joe Sonken's place in Hollywood and feel eyes on her. Playing a role and enjoying it. It was real.

Julie was married to a film stuntman. She was working and couldn't come to the wedding, but wrote a long letter of love and congratulations that ended with, "I knew you had it in you somewhere, you devil. Wow! *My* Mom!"

Karen's mother, only nine years older than Frank, came to the wedding, drank champagne and said, very seriously, "But he's Italian, isn't he?" Her mother went home, and Karen went home three years later for her mother's funeral.

What was going on? Everybody dying. The first Frank and her father, then her mother and the second Frank. Feeling close to so many people for years and then feeling alone, the survivor. Losing touch with old friends in Detroit. Living a different life. Having no one to talk to with any degree of intimacy. Anxious to meet people, have at least one close friend. Preferably a man.

She became more aware of the retired older people in Florida. More women than men in the high-rises that lined the beaches north and south of Lauderdale. Women driving alone in four-door sedans. Women having dinner with other women. Karen was forty-four. She said, I don't look like those women.

Do I?

No, even after all the hours in the sun, tennis in the sun, lying in the sun, she was five-four, weighed exactly one hundred and five and looked ten years younger than her age. Or maybe thirty-eight or -nine; right in there somewhere. With sort of classic good looks: dark hair, blue eyes, nice nose; facial lines that gave her a somewhat drawn look but, Karen told herself, showed character or wisdom or experience. She wore simple but expensive clothes, dressed more often, in the past year, without a bra and looked outstanding, tan and lean, in any of several faded bikinis. God, no, she didn't look like those widows with their gaudy prints and queen-size asses.

Okay, but then what was she doing sitting home alone? Why did the few interesting, eligible men she had met since Frank's death show up once or twice and then seem to vanish?

2.

In May, five months a widow—exactly a year from the time of the double-standard disagreement, the argument with Frank, the ultimatum—Karen was seated in Ed Grossi's private office on the thirty-ninth floor of the Biscayne Tower.

The sign on the double-door entrance to the suite said DORADO MANAGEMENT CORPORATION.

Karen could ask Ed Grossi what Dorado Management managed and he would tell her, oh, apartment buildings, condominiums; that much would probably be true. She could ask him who all the men were, waiting in the lobby, and Grossi would say, oh, suppliers, job applicants, you know. His tone patient. Ask anything. What do you want to know?

But if she were to probe, keep asking questions, she knew from experience the explanation that began simply would become complicated, involved, the words never describing a clear picture.

They sat with glossy-black ceramic coffee mugs on his clean desk, and Karen listened as Grossi said, "Well, it looks like you're worth approximately four million."

Karen said, "Really?" Noncommittal. She had thought it might be much more.

"There was a tax lien that had to be straightened out, some business interests of Frank's sold—I won't go into all that unless you want me to."

Four million.

She still had nearly two hundred thousand of her own in stocks and savings, plus the thirty-five thousand cash—in one hundred dollar bills—she had found in Frank's file cabinet.

"Do I get it in a lump sum?"

Ed Grossi seemed alone and far away on the other side of the clean desk, the Miami Beach skyline behind him, through a wall of glass. Mild Ed Grossi sitting on top of it all. He wore black, heavy-framed glasses and was holding them in a way to see through the bifocal area clearly, looking down at a single sheet of paper on his desk.

"According to the way Frank set it up, the money's held in trust."

"Oh," Karen said, and waited for the complicated explanation.

"In Miami General Revenue bonds, four million at six percent, two hundred and forty thousand a year. How's that sound?"

"Do I pay tax on it?"

"No, they're municipal bonds, the earnings are tax-free. Two-forty or, the way it's set up, twenty thousand a month as long as you live."

Karen waited. There was a catch, she felt sure, certain stipulations. "What if I want to take the entire two hundred and forty thousand, all at once?"

"And do what?"

"I don't know. I'm saying what if. Are the bonds in my name?"

"No, Dorado Management. You remember the lawyer explaining it? Frank appointed Dorado administrator of his estate."

"I thought he appointed you," Karen said.

"No, the corporation. Answer your question, yes, you can take the entire two hundred forty thousand for a given year in one payment but, for your own protection, it would have to be approved by Dorado Management."

"By you," she said again, insisting.

"Karen, I could cross Flagler Avenue and get hit by a car. The corporation is still the administrator of Frank's estate. You follow me? Like as a service to you."

"Then I can't just cash in the bonds if I want and take the four million."

"Why would you want to?" Quietly, with an almost weary sound. "Put it in what? Some hotshot comes along with a scheme—that's why Frank set it up like this. Dorado administrates the capital, does your paperwork, you don't have to worry about it."

"What about when I die?"

"It stops. Your heirs are yours, not Frank's. But, in the meantime you get this money working for you, you'll have quite a sizable estate."

"What if I marry again?"

Ed Grossi hesitated. She saw him, for part of a moment, unprepared.

"I think it stops."

"You're not sure?"

"I don't recall. Maybe Dorado Management has to approve. I don't mean it like that, like you have to get permission. I mean in that case we'd have to assign the bonds to you, if there's no stipulation against it."

"Why would there be?"

"I'm not saying there is. I just don't recall all the details, how it's set up. Why?"

"Why what?"

"I mean are you interested in somebody?"

"No. Not at the moment. I've barely seen anyone," Karen said, with a little edge now in her tone. "I just want to know what my rights are, what I'm allowed to do and what I'm not."

"It was Frank's money, Karen."

"And I earned a share"—still with the edge—"wife subject to the husband, faithfully living up to my end—if you want to make it sound like a legal contract."

"Hey, Karen—come on."

She didn't say anything, but continued to look at him.

"He's dead, Karen. You want him to come back and apologize? The man left you a house, couple of other places, quarter a million a year tax-free— What do you want?"

"I don't know. I feel . . . tied down. Maybe I should get away for a few months."

Ed Grossi hesitated again, forming the right words or a relaxed tone. He said, "You don't have to run off, do you? Get involved in something here, some kind of club activity. Spend your money, enjoy it."

"You sound like Frank."

"That's very possible," Grossi said. "Frank and I were together a long time. He says something, this is his wish, then it's my wish, too. You understand what I mean?"

Karen was watching him, not sure, hoping he would say more and reveal something of himself.

"I don't have to agree with Frank entirely about something," Grossi said. "But he let me know this is the way he wants it, okay, it's the way it's gonna be. What I feel—well, it's got nothing to do with it, it was his business."

Karen waited.

"What're you trying to say?"

"Nothing. I'm repeating myself." Serious, then making an effort to smile as he pressed a button on his intercom. "What else can I do for you, Karen?"

Almost telling her something, how he felt. Then aware of it and backing off.

There had been no interruptions, no phone calls, until Grossi's secretary came in and asked if they'd like more coffee. Karen said thanks, no, and picked up her handbag from the floor. The secretary said, "Roland is here."

"Tell him to wait," Grossi said. He took Karen by surprise then. He said, "Vivian, you know Mrs. DiCilia? Karen, this is Vivian Arzola."

The secretary extended her hand to Karen and smiled. "I'm very pleased to meet you, Mrs. DiCilia. I've heard so much about you."

Like what? Karen wondered, still surprised; and yet she knew the girl meant it.

A very attractive Cuban girl about thirty, neatly

tailored, hair pulled back in a bun, large round glasses, a beige pants suit Karen decided was a Calvin Klein or a Dalby. Vivian seemed to linger. She said, "You are much more beautiful than your picture."

Beautiful? Karen raised her brows to show a little surprise. She said, "Well, thank you. I think I'll come back more often."

Vivian left them, and Grossi said, "What do you need? Anything at all."

Karen settled back. "Why don't you want me to go away? Do I have to have permission?"

"No, of course not. I didn't mean it that way. I'm suggesting why don't you take it easy. Anywhere you go now it's hot. Stay here by the ocean. But keep in touch. Let me know what you're doing and if I can help in any way."

"I'll tell you right now what I'm doing," Karen said. "Nothing. I see someone two or three times—like Howard Shaw, do you know him? He's an investment consultant, belongs to Palm Bay, recently divorced—"

Grossi was shaking his head. "Karen, you've only been a widow, what, a few months. What's the rush?"

"Almost six months," Karen said, "half a year. I've gone out to dinner a few times—Ed, I'm not jumping in bed with anybody. I've been out with three different men that I like, I mean as friends. We have a good time, we seem to get along. They say they'll call tomorrow or in a couple of days, then nothing, not a word."

"I don't know," Grossi said. "Give it time."

"Give what time?"

"Relax, don't worry about it."

Karen waited, staring at him. "Ed, what's going on?"

"You mean, what's going on? They're businessmen, they're busy. Maybe they're out of town."

"They're not out of town. I've seen them."

"Well, their wives found out. I don't know."

"They're not married." Karen waited again. "Is it because I was married to Frank DiCilia?"

"Some people," Grossi said and shrugged. "Who knows."

"I've thought about that," Karen said. "But they knew it, every one of them. I mean I didn't tell them and then they stopped calling. They *knew* I was Mrs. Frank DiCilia. It's my name. It didn't seem to bother them."

"Well, you don't know," Grossi said. "A guy's a lightweight, sooner or later it shows. He gets nervous, starts to look around; he thinks, Jesus Christ, maybe I'm over my head. You understand? Just the idea, going out with Mrs. Frank DiCilia."

Karen didn't say anything.

"If I were you I wouldn't worry about it," Grossi said. "You got everything. What do you need some lightweight for? Right?"

Roland Crowe stepped over from the reception desk to hold the door open for Karen. She said, "Thank you," and Roland said, "Hey, don't mention it." He stood hip-cocked in his tight pants and two-hundred dollar cowboy boots watching her ass and slim brown legs move down the hall. When he turned, letting the door close, all the guys in the Dorado lobby were looking at him. Roland winked at nobody in particular. Bunch of dinks, waiting around for the grass to grow.

He went back to the desk to pick up fooling around with the little receptionist, but she told him he could go in now. Roland gave her a wink, too. She wasn't bad looking for a Cuban. That DiCilia woman wasn't bad looking either. He remembered her face.

In Grossi's office, Roland Crowe said, "Wasn't that Frank's woman just went out?"

Grossi was putting a sheet of paper in his middle desk drawer. He took out another single sheet that bore a name and a street address written in ink and locked the drawer.

"Was that who?"

"Frank's old lady."

"Her name's Mrs. DiCilia," Grossi said.

Shit. Little guinea trying to sound like a hardtimer, bit off words barely moving his mouth, more like he had a turd or something in there. Roland felt sociable—back in Miami after six months at Lake Butler State Prison, busting his ass chopping weeds, eating that slop chow—he felt too good to act mean, though he visualized picking the little guinea up by his blue suit and throwing him through the window—grinning then—hearing his guinea scream going down thirty-nine floors to Biscayne Boulevard.

"I met her one time about, I don't know, a year ago," Roland Crowe said, "I took something out to their house. Frank introduced us, but she don't remember me."

"Here," Grossi said, handing the sheet to Roland who frowned looking at the name.

"Arnold . . . Rapp? What kinda name's that?"

Grossi's expression remained patient, solemn. "Address's up in Hallandale."

"Hiding out, Jesus Christ, in Hallandale," Roland said. "This dink know what he's doing or's he one of them college boys?"

"Arnold tells us the Coast Guard impounded the boat, turned nine tons of grass over to Customs. We see in the paper, yes, there was a boat, Cuban crew, pulled into Boca Chica two days ago."

"But was it Arnold's?" Roland said. "What'd you bank him for?"

"Five hundred forty grand, two and a half to one."

"Well," Roland said, "if he's telling a story he must've smoked a ton of it to get the nerve, huh?"

"Ask him," Grossi said. "The other matter, Mrs. DiCilia, Vivian'll tell you." He reached over to punch a key on the intercom box. "Vivian, Roland's coming out."

Like that, their business over with. There was no, "How was Lake Butler?" or "Thank you, Roland," for keeping his mouth shut, standing up to that asshole judge and drawing a year and day reduced to six months for contempt of court, having to live up there with all them niggers and Cubans.

Roland said to Ed Grossi, "Oh, how'd I make it up at Butler? Well, just fine, Ed. I kept my hands on my private parts, broke a boy's arm tried to cop my joint and came out a two hundred and five pound virgin. I lost some weight on that special diet of grits and hog shit they got."

Ed Grossi said, "Vivian's waiting for you."

"He's going to take so much and then fire you, you know it?" Vivian said.

Roland Crowe gave her a nice grin going over to the glass-top table where she was sitting, a place to talk away from her desk. Roland liked the setup, the glass, looking down through it at Vivian's crossed legs, the thin beige material tight over her thigh. He said, "You know what I kept dreaming about and seeing in my mind all the time I was at Butler? Cuban pussy. Man, all that black hair—"

Vivian said, "I know one Cuban *cocha* you never going to see. Sit down, Roland. Be nice."

He put his hand on his fly as if to unzip his pants. "Come on, you show me yours and I'll show you something you never seen down on Sou'west Eighta Street."

"Sou-wa-SAY-da," Vivian said. "Dumb shit, you never get it right. Come out of the swamp, what, twenty years ago, you still don't know nothing."

"I know I can make you happy," Roland said, having fun, sitting down now and laying his solid forearms on the glass. The cuffs of his flowered shirt were turned back once to show his two-thousand dollar wristwatch and gold ID bracelet. "See, I got to find a new place. I thought I'd move in with you while I was looking."

"That's what I need in my life, a convict," Vivian said. She was straight with Roland but very careful and alert, as though he might slam a fist down on the glass table, and she would have to get out of there fast. She said, "You ready to listen, quit the bullshit?"

What he'd like to do was reach over and take off Vivian's big round glasses and pull her hair loose, but he said, "Sure. Tell me about it." Roland felt really good and could be obliging for awhile.

"Mrs. Frank DiCilia, One Isla Bahía, Harbor Beach, Lauderdale."

"I been to the house."

"There's a tap on the phone line that goes into Marta's room from outside—"

"Wait a minute. Who's Marta?"

"Marta Diaz, the maid. Sister of Jesus." Vivian pronounced the name Hay-soos.

Roland said, "Sweet Jesus working on this?" and pronounced it Jesus. "I never knew he had a sister. I never knew *what* he had. He don't talk hardly at all."

Vivian said, "Listen, all right? The recorder is in Marta's room. Every night she takes the cassette out and gives it to Jesus."

"Then what?"

"Then—he was bringing it here, but now he gives it to you and you listen to it. You write down the names of men she talks to. If it looks like she's got something going with one of them, you find out about him, go see him, tell him Mrs. DiCilia would like to be left alone. You understand? You don't hit anyone unless you ask us first."

"For how long?"

Vivian shrugged. "Long as she lives, I don't know. She's not to see anyone in a serious way that she might go to bed with."

Roland squinted, like he was looking into sunglare. "Grossi want her for himself?"

"It's not his idea, it's the husband's."

"The man's dead." Still squinting.

"Is that right? But people still do what he wants," Vivian said. "He wants his wife to remain pure, true to him even after death, and we see to it."

"That's a good looking woman," Roland said.

"Yes, very stylish."

"And she's not getting anything? Jesus, she must be dying."

"Everyone isn't a sex maniac," Vivian said.

"You don't have to be wild with the notion to want some poon." Roland saw the poor woman alone in her house at night, looking out the window. "Maybe she has some boy sneak in, give her a jump."

Vivian shook her head. "Marta says no one stays, they don't go in the bedroom."

Roland was thinking, You don't have to do it in the bedroom. Shit, he'd done it in a car trunk, in sand, weeds, an air boat in the middle of Big Cyprus Swamp, one time right on the Seventy-ninth Street Causeway like she was sitting on the railing . . . on floors—all kinds of floors, carpet, linoleum—on a table— He'd never done it on a glass table though.

Roland wanted to get it straight in his mind. "This is Frank's idea not Ed's."

"Like he left it in his will to Ed," Vivian said. "Watch her so she doesn't fool around with anyone, ever."

"Jesus—" It was a hard proposition to understand, cutting the poor woman off like that. But then these guineas did all kinds of things that didn't make sense. Serious little buggers with their old-timey ideas about honor, the *omerta*—no talking, man, keep your mouth shut—all that brotherhood bullshit.

Roland said, "It seems to me, an easier way—why don't Ed tell her, no fooling around. Here's what Frank wants, dead or not, and that's the way it's gonna be."

"Why do you ask questions?" Vivian said. "Ed doesn't like the idea but he's doing it, uh? For his friend."

"But he doesn't want her to know."

"He doesn't want to be involved," Vivian said. "The woman's also a friend. He wants her to be happy, but he has to do this to her. So he gives it to you because he gave his word to Frank. But he doesn't want to be in*volv*ed in it personally. You understand now? God."

"Who knows about the setup?"

"The three of us. See, he doesn't even want to hear himself tell you about it. I have to tell you."

"What about Jesus? He knows."

"No, he thinks the woman is being protected."

Roland liked that idea. He thought about it some more and said, "What'd Frank leave her?"

"None of your business."

"I bet a big shit-pile of money," Roland said. "And I bet that's part of the deal. She starts putting out, she gets cut off, huh?"

"Pick up the tapes and listen to them," Vivian said. "That's all you got to do." She rose from the table to walk over to her desk. It was not clean like Ed Grossi's, it was a working desk with papers and file folders on it. Vivian picked up an envelope that was thick and sealed closed, no writing on it.

"Protect her," Roland was saying, nodding, accepting the idea. "Keep all these dinks away from her who want to get in her little panties. All right, I guess I can do that."

Vivian came back with the envelope and handed it to him, saying, "Roland"—reading his mind, which wasn't difficult—"while you're protecting her little panties, don't try to get in them yourself. I told you, she's a very good friend of Ed's."

"We're all friends," Roland said, ripping open the envelope, "that's why we get along so good." He looked at the money, counting through it quickly, then at Vivian. "I don't get any extra? Shit, I just did six months at Butler, hard time, lady, and I pick up my paycheck as usual, huh?"

"Join a union," Vivian said. "What're you complaining to me for? You got eighteen thousand dollars there, back pay for your six months."

"The way I see it, chopping weeds at Butler is worth more than that," Roland said. "Way more."

3.

During the time Maguire was being held in the Wayne County Jail, downtown Detroit, he'd say to himself, If I get out of this—sometimes even beginning, Please, God, if I get out of this I'll change, I'll get a regular job, I'll stay away from people like the Patterson brothers and never fuck up again as long as I live. At least not this bad.

Sitting there in his cell facing something like 15 to 25, Jesus, the scaredest he'd ever been in his life.

While over at the prosecutor's office they could push computer buttons and Maguire would appear in lights on the desk-set screen.

CALVIN A. MAGUIRE, Male Caucasian, a date of birth that made him thirty-six, tatoo on his upper left bicep, *Cal,* in blue and red, a list of arrests going back eleven years, one in Florida, but no convictions.

An assistant Wayne County prosecutor looked at the screen, frowning. No convictions? The guy had stolen automobiles, broken into homes, business establishments, once attempted to shoot a man, apprehended with a concealed weapon, one willful destruction . . . and no con*vic*tions? Well, they had the guy this time. Two eyeball witnesses who'd picked him out of a line-up, two positive IDs, man. Calvin Maguire was going away.

The prosecutor's office also had an impressive computerized light show on the Patterson brothers: Andre Patterson and Grover "Cochise" Patterson, both male Negroes, both with previous convictions going back to ages thirteen and fourteen, and both picked out of line-ups by the same two tight-jawed no-bullshit witnesses. Bye-bye Maguire and the Patterson brothers. The assistant prosecutor was going to trial happy. He didn't see how he could lose.

Andre Patterson had come to Maguire with the deal. This man was going to pay them fifteen hundred each to go and take a hit at the Deep Run Country Club out north of Detroit. Mess the place up, but mostly mess up their minds, the people out there. Maguire didn't get it. A man was paying them to hit a place?

Paying them and furnishing clean weapons. The man had some reason he didn't like the place, or he wanted to pay them back for something, not anybody in particular, the whole place. Maguire said, At a club they *sign* for everything; there's no money at a club. Andre Patterson said, But the rich people who go there have money; put it in their locker, go out and play golf. See, they could keep whatever they took. The man didn't want a cut; it wasn't that kind of deal.

Maguire was uncertain. What's the matter with your buddies Ordell and Louis? Why me? And Andre answering that those two were away for a while. No, you my man, only man I know can do it cool, without a nosefull. Maguire told Andre he was doing fine without the thrills; he had a job he thought he'd stick with at least until the end of the year, then take off.

Andre Patterson saying, Yeah, making the *cock*tails for the salesmen flashing around the hotel, listening to all the big deals, the *cock*tail music coming out the wall, standing at attention in your little red jacket, man, hair combed nice, yes sir, what would you like? And for the young lady?

Maguire thinking of a snowbanked Durant Mall in Aspen, deep powder on the high slopes, the rich ladies in their snow-bunny outfits. Then thinking of the Pier House in Key West, sitting out on the deck with a white rum and lemon, six in the evening. Places out of the past. Thinking of fifteen hundred bucks and what they could scrounge out of the lockers, maybe two three hundred more each. Thinking of islands and palm trees . . . get out of the cold, the slush, try the Mediterranean for a change, Spain, the south of France. Fifteen hundred guaranteed. Maguire liked to be outdoors. He liked to work outdoors, if he had to work. What was he doing in Detroit? Like a guilt trip, always coming back to Detroit, visit his mom and tell her yeah, everything was great. Listen to her describe her poor circulation and Detroit Edison rates and finally saying, Hey, thanks very much for everything, accepting the hundred dollar bill she always offered and getting out of there.

Andre Patterson saying, No security people. Walk in, pick up the wallets, watches. All right, everybody take off your clothes, get in the shower. Carry their clothes outside and throw 'em in the bushes—they all running around the club nekked.

Maybe wear ski masks, something like that?

Andre saying, Wear a tuxedo you want to. We going to the *club,* man.

That would be funny, tuxedos. It was good to keep it light, have a couple of drinks, smoke a joint before going in . . . lock the outside door after you . . . little details to think about. Watch the door that went from the locker room to the grill—

Maguire said, "I haven't done this in a couple years. I mean I haven't *ever* actually done it, Christ, gone into a country club."

Andre said, "Who has?"

They went in on a Wednesday, August 16, four o'clock in the afternoon, when all the doctors and sales reps would be out there playing golf, rolling Indian dice for drinks, talking their locker room talk with all the obscene words they couldn't say at the office.

They parked the van Cochise had picked up and went in a side door that led directly into the men's locker room—without the ski masks, too hot—Andre Patterson wearing a knit cap and faking some kind of Jamaican-Caribbean British-nigger accent, Cochise wearing a red and white polka-dot headband that bunched up his Afro like black broccoli. Maguire had quit his job at the hotel cocktail lounge, had a photograph taken for his passport application, then let his dark, black-Irish beard grow for three days. Once in the locker room he picked up a green Deep Run golf cap and set it on low over his sunglasses. He and Andre carried 9mm Berettas, brand new; wild-ass Cochise went in with a sawed-off double-barreled Marlin to scare the shit out of the members, get their attention quick and make them behave.

Maguire was nervous going in, Christ yes, but he wasn't too worried about the Patterson brothers overreacting, becoming vicious. There was a moment right in the beginning when they either grabbed control of the situation and it went smoothly, or they didn't grab control and it could turn into a fuck-up with a lot of yelling and jabbing. That moment of surprise—

The golf club members talking loud, their voices coming from the shower and the rows of lockers, middle-aged men in their underwear and towels, shuffling around in paper slippers . . . looking up and seeing, Christ, a wildman, a Mau-Mau, twin blunt holes of a Marlin pointing at them, Oh, my God! Sharp little startled sounds, seeing *two* mean-looking black guys with guns—

Then silence.

God Almighty, was it a revolution or a holdup? Hoping all they wanted was money. Andre Patterson telling the members in Jamaican to be cool, mon, and go in the shower room. Herding those wide-eyed, slow-moving white bodies in there, guns touching naked flesh—go on, mon, move your chickenfat ass—like a scene in a high-class concentration camp, moving them into the gas chamber. Getting the shit-scared locker room attendant to start opening up the lockers. Cochise going through the shoeshine room and the service bar into the ladies locker room—yeah, let's get everybody in here—the three of them actually grinning. Sure, because they knew they had it in their hands now. Unbelievable, Maguire thought, relaxing a little, already seeing himself and the Patterson brothers talking about it after, laughing, giggling at the scene, retelling parts of it one or the other might have missed

Maguire dumping the clubs out of the golf bag, hanging it over his shoulder and throwing in all the wallets and watches, silver money clips with the club crest, a few pinkie rings, electric razors, hair-blower for Cochise—all the stuff he got out of the lockers. Unbelievable, the doctors and sales reps contributing something over twenty-five hundred in cash, like eight-fifty apiece.

Still talking about it the next day at Andre's, eating Chinese food, reading about it in the paper, ARMED TRIO ROBS COUNTRY CLUB. Bet to it, cleaned it out. All those chickenfat doctors out on the links, a man lining up a putt not knowing at that moment he was getting robbed.

They had fun talking about it. Maguire borrowed Andre's car, picked up his photos and a passport application at the post office, brought back some more scotch, shaved, cleaned up, and they went over the scenes again, waiting now for the man to send them the fifteen hundred each.

Talking about Cochise bringing the five women in through the service bar from the ladies locker room on the other side. Four ladies going to fat, holding their towels up around their titties. One not too bad, nice blonde, quiet, fairly calm, Maguire might've set up for a drink at some other time. Cochise pulling the towel off the last one, hearing her squeal as he poked her in the ass with the cut-down Marlin.

That was the highlight, making them all drop their towels or take off their extra-size undies once they were in the shower with the men. The men standing there trying to hold in their stomachs, looking at the bare-naked ladies, at their big titties and bushes. So that's what so-and-so looks like without any clothes on, Jesus. Looking, making little mental notes. Couple of the women sneaking glances at the guy's shriveled-up joints. The shower room full of bellies and dimpled asses that looked like they'd been kept in a dark cave for years.

Andre Patterson saying, "I advise you all to go join Vic Tanney quick as you can, else you gonna die soon." Then saying to a little guy with muscles in his arms and shoulders, who kept staring at Andre, not interested in the naked ladies, "Don't do what you're thinking, man, or you gonna die right now."

See, relaxed but very alert.

Cochise bringing in the two waitresses and the bartender, making them take their uniforms off and get in with the naked club members. Andre saying, Hey, I can't tell the rich folks from the help. Funny guys, half-stoned but they knew what they were doing.

Maguire saying, "Something like that, you could sell tickets to, you know it? I mean there some people would *pay* to see a show like that, fucking X-rated stick-up."

Maguire picking out a set of woods for himself, Andre taking a whole big bag of clubs that must've been worth eight hundred dollars, he said for playing at Palmer Park. Hey, shit, can you see it?

Sometime during the evening of the day after, Cochise went out to pick up some grass, trade in some of the country club items maybe.

He came back with about eighteen members of the Detroit Police Department, Christ, through the door with guns and kneeling on them before they knew what was happening.

So there was the robbery armed, something like 15 to 25 or possibly life, and a felony-firearm charge that carried a mandatory two years. More than enough to start Maguire praying and making promises in the Wayne County jail. In there from the middle of August to the end of November, with no way in the world of making the bond set at fifty thousand dollars or two sureties. Maguire saw Andre and Cochise once at 1300 Beaubien, police headquarters across the street, while they were waiting to appear in a line-up, and asked him, For Christ sake, the man got us into this, he's gonna put up the bond, right? No, the man couldn't get involved just yet. The man was under suspicion, using the bonding company to front him on some kind of deal in Las Vegas, so the man couldn't be seen to be paying the bonding company at this time. But hang on.

Hang onto what, for Christ sake? Hang on in the bus going to Jackson.

Maguire didn't think much of his court-appointed lawyer because the lawyer didn't think much of him. Maguire could feel it, the guy was going through the motions. The court was paying the lawyer, and he didn't give a rat's ass who won.

Maguire said, "What've they got on me? Some circumstantial evidence, that's all."

"Your photograph in Andre Patterson's car," the lawyer said. "The golf clubs in the trunk."

"I happened to leave my picture in the car"—shit—"that was the next day. Other people were in that car the next day. Andre's wife, she went out to get some Chinese food. Was she arrested?"

"You were ID-ed positively in a line-up by one of the victims," the lawyer said. "Possibly identified by four more. They saw you there. Now I'm representing you, not the jigs. You want to agree to testify against the jigs, maybe I can get you a deal."

"You can get fucked, too," Maguire told his court-appointed lawyer. What a rotten guy.

Something happened, several things, Maguire didn't understand.

The morning of the trial a different lawyer appeared in court to defend all three of them, a sharp young guy by the name of Marshall Fine, with styled hair and a pinched-in three-piece suit.

What's this?

Nice moves, very stylish; made the prosecutor look like a high-school football coach. Sent from the man? Andre nodding, pleased. Fine of fine and dandy, man.

From the company does the man's legal business. Yeah, but the guy seemed so young. Was he practicing on them, or what? Maguire wasn't sure he liked it—putting his life in the hands of a young Jewish lawyer who looked about eighteen years old. He hoped to Christ the guy was an authentic hotshot young Jewish lawyer and not just somebody's nephew.

Marshall Fine didn't say much that morning, accepting the jurors one right after the other, very calm, courteous, but maybe wanting to get it over with. In the afternoon, first thing, the prosecutor put a witness on the stand. Oh shit, the little guy from the shower room with the muscles in his arms and shoulders—the guy describing what happened and saying yes, he saw the three in the courtroom, the white guy there and the two colored guys.

Marshall Fine got up and asked the club member where he was standing, in front or behind the others, what exactly took place during the incident and, in all that confusion, he couldn't be absolutely certain of his identification, could he?

Yes, the club member said, he could definitely be certain. He not only saw them in the locker room, he saw the white guy's picture a few days later when the police officer showed it to him.

Marshall Fine asked the club member what picture. Maguire noticed the prosecutor paying very close attention, frowning.

The club member said he was told the picture was found in their car.

Pictures of all three defendants?

No, just the white guy, the club member said. The officer showed it to him when he came down to 1300 Beaubien to look at the suspects.

Marshall Fine said, to no one in particular, "While Mr. Maguire was being held in custody." Then to the judge, "Your Honor, I'd like to request, if I may, the jury be excused. We seem to have a legal point to discuss."

Twenty minutes later Maguire was free. He couldn't believe it.

Marshall explained it to him in the hall, with all the people standing around outside the courtrooms, and Maguire had trouble concentrating. *Free,* just like that.

"What it amounts to, the cops fucked up. Once you're in jail they can't show anybody your picture unless your lawyer's present."

"They can't?"

"See, it used to be the cops would tell the victim, or a witness, they got the guy and then show the guy's picture. Then, when the witness sees the guy in the line-up, naturally he's gonna pick him out, the same guy, of course."

Maguire nodding—

"The prosecutor raised the point, this impermissible taint, what it's called in law, was irrelevant because there was an independent basis for the identification. I said what independent basis? Like knowing you from someplace else. I pointed out there was absolutely no independent corroboration that would provide a sufficiently acceptable al*ter*native identification that comports with due process. And the judge agreed. It was that simple."

"Oh," Maguire said.

"So, good luck. Get your ass out of here." Young Marshall Fine turned to go back into the courtroom, then stopped. "I almost forgot. You need a job? What're you gonna do now?"

There it was. "I got some money coming in," Maguire said.

"I don't know anything about that," the lawyer said. "I guess I'm only into rehabilitation, small favors, maybe something we might be able to do for you. Were you working?"

"I was a bartender, but I quit."

"I could get you something like that. How about Miami Beach?"

"Well"—seeing the black people standing around, all the victims, witnesses, relatives of defendants—"I used to live in Florida about ten years ago." Thinking in that moment, the Mediterranean, Florida, what's the difference? Seeing himself going to the cops to get his passport pictures back? No way. "Yeah, Florida sounds like a good idea."

"Get you into one of the hotels, bartender—what do you want to do?"

Thinking of the ocean, the sun, being outside, getting a tan—

"When I was there before I worked with dolphins. Maybe something like that'd be good." He felt funny talking to a guy younger than he was about a job.

"Dolphins," Marshall said.

"Porpoise. You know, they call them porpoise but they're really dolphins. Not the fish, they're mammals."

"Yeah, dolphins," Marshall said. He was nodding, thinking of something. "I believe we've got a client—yeah, I'm sure we have—they've got an interest in one of those places. You mean like Sea World, they put on the porpoise show, a guy rides a killer whale, Shamu?"

"Yeah, only the place I worked," Maguire said, "it was more a training school. Down in the Keys, with these pens right out in the ocean. They put on a show, but not with all the bullshit, the porpoise playing baseball and, you know, coming out of the water to ring a bell and the American flag goes up—not any of that kind of shit."

"But you've had experience."

"I worked there almost a year, down on Marathon. The pay wasn't anything, but I liked being outside." He thought about the fifteen hundred again. "What about this money somebody owes me?"

"I'm sorry, I don't know anything about it." The young hotshot lawyer did seem to want to help though. "You must've made some kind of an arrangement."

"Well, I guess so. But then some snitch sees Cochise walking in a place with a golf bag full of electric razors and that's it. We were picked up, you know, before anything was paid."

"I don't know anything about it, so don't ask, okay? But I'll see where we stand with the porpoise. You say porpoise or porpoises, plural?"

"Either way," Maguire said.

"Nice clean animals," Marshall said. "Give me a call in a couple of days." He turned to go back into the courtroom.

"What about the Pattersons? You think you can get 'em off?"

"I don't lose if I can win," Marshall said. He paused, hand on the door. "It's too bad they didn't pull the kind of dumb stunt you did, leave some snapshots in the car. I'll see you."

Andre and Grover Patterson drew 20 to life.

A few days before they were sentenced, Maguire gave Andre's wife a list of things to tell Andre and two questions, in particular, to ask him, when she went into see him on visitor's day.

She came out of the Wayne County jail, Maguire waiting, and they walked the three blocks south to Monroe, Greektown, for a cup of coffee.

Andre's wife said, "Yeah, he understand. You out and he's in, that's all. That dumb, stupid man"—shaking her head, sounding tired—"he's always in. Must miss his friends at Jackson so much, got to get back to them."

"You tell him I got a job waiting for me, but I want to do something first?"

"Yeah, I told him."

"I'm gonna write to him all about it. And give you his money? You tell him that?"

"I told him."

"Good." Maguire sipped his coffee. "And you asked him the man's name? He told me once, but I wasn't sure. I might've got it mixed up with somebody else."

"Yeah, the man's name is Frank DiCilia," Andre's wife said.

"That's it." Maguire nodded. Right, Frank DiCilia. He knew it was something like Cecilia or Cadelia. Years ago the name had been in the papers a lot.

"And how about where he lives? Or where I get in touch with him?"

"His home's in Florida—"

"Is that right?" Maguire perking up. "That's where I'm going, Florida." Maybe it was a sign, things beginning to come together without a lot of sweat and strain. "Where, Miami Beach?"

"Fort something. Fort Laura—"

"Fort Lauderdale."

"Yeah, Fort Lauradale."

Jesus, it *was* a sign. That's where he was going for the job. The man was right there. No special trip required. It would give him time to think about it, how to approach a man like Frank DiCilia. Show him the clipping from the paper, TRIO ROBS COUNTRY CLUB, identify himself as one of the defendants—

"But ain't no way you gonna see him," Andre's wife said.

"What do you mean? Why not?"

"The man died about a week ago," Andre's wife said. "Andre say he heard about it. You didn't?"

4.

Some of Roland Crowe's buddies were still sloshing around back there in the swamp, driving air boats, guiding hunting and fishing parties, poaching alligators, making shine; some others were doing time at Raford and Lake Butler. Bunch of dinks.

Roland had been that entire route and had poured cement for five years before going broke and learning the simple secret of success in business. Deal only in personal services. Not *things*. No lifting, no heavy work, no overhead, no machinery to speak of. Look good, listen carefully, take a minimum of shit, live close to the Beach and always make yourself available to people who called and said, Roland, there's this man owes us money. Or, Roland, we believe this man is going independent on us. Or, we believe he's telling us a story . . .

Like the guy laying-up at Hallandale, Arnold Rapp. Financed him like a half million dollars, and he says the Coast Guard confiscated the shipment, nine tons of Columbian.

Say, Come on, Arnold, for true? Holding him out the window by his ankles.

Get that done, then stop by Lauderdale on the way back and say hi to the DiCilia lady. Look the situation over, lay in some footings.

First thing though, Roland spent his back pay. He bought himself four new summer suits the man told him were designed in Paris, France, and specially cut for them by this tailor in Taiwan, Republic of China. He bought himself new three-hundred-fifty-dollar hand-tooled, high-heeled boots. He bought an Ox Bow wheat-colored straw hat with a high crown and a big scoop brim that, with the cowboy boots, put him up around six-six. He bought a cream-colored Cadillac Coupe d'Ville, cash. And put two months' rent down on an eight hundred dollar apartment in Miami Shores.

Look good and you feel good. He picked up Jesus Diaz and drove up to Hallandale.

"I bet what it is," Roland said to Jesus, "I bet anything Arnold is a boy went to about five colleges, traveled all over, got busted a couple of times, has his rich folks bail him out and he thinks he's a fucking outlaw. You think I'm wrong?"

"No, you right," Jesus Diaz said. He was comfortable in the air-conditioned Cadillac, he didn't want to argue with Roland.

"See, they get together, these snotty boys like Arnold? They think shit, they been to college, dumb guineas financing the deal don't know nothing. Tell 'em the load went down the toilet and keep the money."

"Maybe so," Jesus Diaz said.

"No maybe. These little shitheads're pulling something." Jesus Diaz did not reply and Roland said, "You don't believe it?"

"I believe it if you want me to," Jesus Diaz said. He knew he should keep still, but he didn't like Roland's bright-blue pimp suit or the big Lone Ranger hat touching the roof of the car. He said, "Why they in business then? They make more selling it, don't they?"

"They *do* sell it, you dink," Roland said. "But they tell Grossi they lost it, and he's out his dough."

"They believe they can get away with that?" Jesus Diaz said.

"Jesus," Roland said, not meaning the little Cuban but the other Jesus. "You should never've gone in the ring, you know it? I think you got your brains scrambled."

Jesus Diaz agreed with that in part. To look like Kid Gavilan and fake a bolo punch wasn't enough. After thirty-seven professional fights, several times getting the shit beat out of him and almost losing an eye, he could still see clearly and think clearly and knew this man next to him was a prehistoric creature from the swamp—man, from some black lagoon—who wore cowboy hats and *chulo* suits and squinted at life to see only what he wanted. Maybe he could punch with Roland and hurt him a little, but before it was over Roland would kill him. Roland's fists were too big and his nose and jaw were up there too far away.

Jesus Diaz, looking up at the green freeway sign as they passed beneath it, almost there now, said, "Hallandale."

"Yeah?" Roland said. "Hallandale. You can read English, huh?"

What Jesus Diaz would like to do, take the man's cowboy hat from his head, reach over and grab it and sail it out the window.

This one, they should keep him locked up someplace with his mouth taped.

Then let him out to do the work, yes, because no one walked into a room and faced people the way Roland did.

Into 410 of the Ocean Monarch high-rise condominium on the beach, Jesus Diaz behind him, into the big living room of the apartment with the expensive furniture, where the four young guys were sitting with their beer cans and music and the smell of grass—a heavy smell even with the sliding door open to the balcony.

Arnold Rapp, the one they came to see, let them in, looked them over, turned and walked back to the couch. Jesus Diaz closed the door behind them. He liked the loud funk-rock music. He didn't like the way the four young guys were at ease and didn't seem to be scared. Yes, stoned, but it was more than that. They lounged, sitting very low in the couch and the chairs, no shoes on, each with long hair. They looked like bums, Jesus Diaz thought, and maybe Roland was right. Rich kids, yes, who didn't give a shit about anything. Man, a place like this, view of the ocean, swimming pool downstairs in the court—these guys laying around drinking beer like they just came off a shift, not offering anything, waiting, like Roland was here to explain something or ask for a job. That was the feeling.

Roland said, "Your mommy home?"

They grinned at him. Arnold said, "No, no mommy, just us kids."

Roland said, "Well now—who're your little friends, Arnie?"

Arnold said, "Well now"—imitating Roland's cracker accent, getting some of the soft twang—"this here is Barry. That there're Scott and Kenny."

The young guys—they were about in their mid-twenties—snickered and giggled.

The one called Barry, trying the accent, said, "And who be you be?"

It broke them up, "Who be you be." The guys laughing and repeating it, Jesus, who-be-you-be. They thought it was pretty funny.

Roland walked over to the hi-fi. He brushed the stylus off the record and the funk-rock stopped with a painful scratching sound.

Arnold straightened up. "Jesus Christ, what're you *do*ing?"

"Getting your attention," Roland said.

Barry was still grinning. He said, "Who-be-you-be, man?" And one of the others said, "He's the who-be-you-be man. Comes in, who-be-you-bes your fucking records all up."

"No, I'm the man's man," Roland said. "Sent me to ask you what happened to his five hundred and forty thousand dollars, I believe is the figure."

"It's in the municipal incinerator," Arnold said.

The one named Barry said, "We already told it, man. Ask him."

Roland tilted up his Ox Bow straw. He walked out to the open balcony with its view of the Atlantic Ocean and leaned on the rail a moment.

Jesus Diaz stood where he was in the middle of the room, watching Roland, hearing the young guys say something and giggle. Something like, "Hey, partner" and something about riding here on a fucking horse, and another one saying, "A fucking bucking bronco, man," and all of them giggling again.

Roland came back in. He said to Arnold, "How about you tell me what you told him."

"Coast Guard picked up the boat in international waters and brought it into Boca Chica," Arnold said. "He knows all that. The pot went to Customs and they burned it up."

"Pot went to pot," Barry said.

"The crew, the three guys, were turned over to Drug Enforcement," Arnold said. "Your man is out the five hundred forty grand and there's nothing I can do about it."

"It's a high fucking risk business," Barry said, "any time you get two hundred percent on your investment, it's got to be."

"Two and a half," Arnold said.

"Right, two and a half," Barry said. "You know it's high risk going in, man, if you're not stupid."

Roland walked over to where Barry was lounged in his chair. He said, "Is that right, little fella? You know all about high risk, do you? Stand up here, let me have a look at you."

"Jesus Christ," Barry said, sounding bored. "Why don't you take a fucking walk?"

Roland pulled Barry up by his hair, drew him out of the chair and an agonized sound from Barry's throat, telling him to hush up, turned him around and got a tight grip on the waist of Barry's pants that brought him to his toes, Levis digging into the crack of his ass.

Jesus Diaz reached behind him, beneath his jacket —to the same place Roland was gripping the young guy's pants—and brought out a Browning automatic, big .45, and put it on the other three guys, sitting up, maybe about to jump Roland.

Roland said, "See it?" without even looking, knowing Jesus had the piece on them. "Now tell me about high risk," Roland said to Barry, walking him toward the open balcony, the other three guys rigid, afraid to move. "You want *me* to tell you?" Roland said, bringing the young guy to the opening in the sliding glass doors. "Fact I'll show you, boy, the highest risk you ever saw." And ran him out on the balcony, gripping him, raising him by his hair and pants and grunting hard as he threw the young guy screaming over the rail of the fourth-floor balcony.

Someone in the room cried out, "Jesus—no!"

There was silence.

Jesus Diaz held the gun on them, not looking at the balcony.

Roland stood at the rail, leaning over it, resting on his arms.

When he came back in adjusting his hat he said, "That boy was lucky, you know it? He hit in the swimming pool. He's moving slow, but he's moving. People gonna say my, what do those boys do up there? Must get all likkered up, huh?" Roland paused, looking at Arnold and Scott and Kenny sitting there like stones. He said, "Now, who-be-you-be, who be's gonna answer my question without getting smart-aleck and giggling like little kids? You see what I do to smart little kids, huh. Next one, he might hit the concrete, mightn' he?"

"The name of the boat in the paper was *Salsa,*" Arnold said quietly. "The same one I hired, I know, because I saw it in Key West two weeks ago."

"And the Coast Guard cutter hauled it in was the *Diligence,*" Roland said. "Same thing I'm gonna use till you pay us back the five hundred and forty thousand. You can take your time, Arnie, we're reasonable folks. Long as you understand the vig's fifty-four grand a week, standard ten percent interest."

Arnold began to nod, very serious. "We'll pay you, don't worry."

Roland said, "Do I look worried?"

He said to Jesus, in the car, driving away from the beach, "I told you, didn't I, them dinks'd pull something."

"But they weren't lying to you," Jesus Diaz said. "It was the same boat was picked up."

"Oh my oh my, you don't understand shit, do you?" Roland drove in silence to the federal highway, US 1, went through the light and pulled over to the curb. "Out you go, partner."

Jesus looked around. "What am I supposed to do here?"

"Hitch a ride or take a cab, I don't give a shit. I'm going up to Lauderdale."

Roland was looking at himself in the rearview mirror, squaring his new Ox Bow wheat-colored straw.

5.

"He say he's a friend of Mr. Grossi," Marta said. "Mr. Grow. You supposed to have met him one time before."

"Crow?" Karen said. She felt Gretchen's tongue on her shoulder. The dog had come out with Marta.

"Yes, Grow," Marta said.

Lying on her stomach, Karen looked at the watch close to her face. Quarter to five already. It amazed her that time did go quickly. Time now to—what? Go in and dress. She didn't remember a Mr. Grow from anywhere. Turning, getting up from the lounge, Karen held the bra of her bathing suit to her breasts, fastened it, then reached for the phone on the umbrella table and dialed a number, Ed Grossi's private line.

"Ed? Karen." She paused, listening a moment. "Everything's fine . . . No, no problems. Listen, do you know someone, a man by the name of Grow? . . . Yeah, that's what I thought. That must be it . . . No, I don't know what he wants. Is he a friend of yours?" Then listened to Ed saying well, yes, in a way. Roland Crowe was an employee. He'd probably stopped by to see if there was anything she needed, maybe take a look around—"For what?" Like a security check, Ed said, that's all. But listen, if the guy was imposing, taking up her time, tell him to get lost. That bluntly. Not someone whose feelings Ed Grossi cared about. "Thanks," Karen said. And Ed said sure, anytime.

Quiet Ed Grossi, trying to sound himself, but a little disturbed. By what? Her call, perhaps interrupting him? Or the fact Roland was here. Whoever Roland

Crowe was. A man who worked for Ed Grossi but wasn't Italian or Cuban.

"Ask him to come out," Karen said. She reached for a white cotton robe as Marta went back to the house.

Roland walked along the seawall to the point of land where a boat canal joined the Intercoastal. He stood for some time looking across the broad channel to the homes on the far side, then turned and seemed to study the DiCilia house: the million dollar layout that resembled a California mission, tan brick and clay tile roof; red pyracantha bushes forming borders, screening the swimming pool and brick patio.

As Roland came this way across the lawn, Karen watching him, Gretchen ran out from the house, barking, coming to a sudden stop. Roland went down to one knee to take the dog in his hands, playfully roughing her up, saying something, repeating it, as the little gray dog licked and sniffed him.

Gretchen ran off toward the house and Roland squinted after her. Coming to the patio he said, "That's a nice little doggie you got. What's her name?"

"Gretchen," Karen said.

"Yeah, she's a nice little girl." Squinting up at the house again, then looking directly at Karen in the canvas chair. "I thought that was some view out there, but this one beats it." Giving her a friendly grin. "I've sure heard a lot about you."

Karen touched her knee to pull the robe over her leg, but let her hand rest there.

Roland caught it, the brown hand with three little gold rings lying there idle on the brown knee. Yes sir, begin small and work up. No hurry. This woman might not even realize how bad she needed it. Like a starving person forgetting about food as the stomach began to shrink up.

Marta was hanging around back there in the shade of one of the archways, door open behind her, leading inside. Roland didn't know if Marta was keeping an eye on him or what. Maybe told by the lady to stay close.

The lady, he figured was near his age, somewhere around forty. The maid, twenty years younger, and with a little more meat on her but not as good looking. Both of them in white. A short-skirt skimpy uniform; and the robe the lady wore, Roland bet, didn't cover no more than a little swim suit. She might even be bare-assed under there. Two women in white all alone in this place like a Florida castle. It sounded to Roland like something in a storybook. The fair princess with some kind of a spell on her that she'd have till her prince come along and fucked her.

All that going on in his head inside the summer cowboy hat. Hey, prince—Roland grinned.

"What's funny?" Karen said.

"Nothing. I was thinking of something." Then serious. "See, the problem, this place is pretty exposed, out here on a point."

"I don't see a problem," Karen said.

"What I mean, the place is tempting. Be easy for somebody to get in here, maybe clean out your jewel box." Roland kept staring at her with a grin fixed on his mouth.

"We have security service, it's around here all night," Karen said.

"Yeah, well those rent-a-cops aren't worth—they're mostly older retired fellas."

"What I don't understand—you walked all around —what exactly you're looking for."

"Any evidence somebody's been setting the place up," Roland said. Was she too thin? Naw, her hips looked a nice size, nice round white curve there. "See, I was originally from over in the Everglades. Used to track, hunt a lot, so I got a fairly keen eye for reading sign."

Karen studied him. She said then, "Would you like something cold?"

"Sure, that'd be fine."

She looked over her shoulder. "Marta? Bring out a couple of vodka and tonic, okay?" And continued to look that way until Marta was in the house. Turning to Roland again, Karen said, "Mr. Grossi didn't ask you to come here."

Roland sank into a canvas director's chair and stretched out his boots, crossing his ankles—fairly close now with kind of a side view of her.

"He didn't?"

"Is this your idea, or did someone send you?"

"My idea, in a way."

"What do you mean, in a way?"

"Coming here is my idea, but I wouldn't be here, would I, if it wasn't for the situation."

"What situation?"

"Your being a widow, the way things've been going and all." Roland teased her with his grin, like he knew more and was holding back. They were getting to the good part quick, and he was enjoying it. This woman sure wasn't dumb.

"What situation exactly are we talking about?" Karen said.

"I'm not allowed to tell."

"But you're going to, aren't you?" Karen said. "Or you wouldn't be here."

She was aware of a curious feeling, wanting to urge him to explain, but knowing she didn't have to. She could sit back, and it would come out. She could show indifference, and he would still tell her.

Roland was squinting with a slight grin. "You figured that out, huh? I'm not just inspecting the premises."

"Well, otherwise you wouldn't have mentioned it," Karen said. "You're certainly not a little kid."

"No, I'm not little," Roland said.

"Sometimes little kids say, 'I've got a secret, and I'm not gonna tell you what it is.' What you said was, you're not sup*pos*ed to tell." Patient, speaking to a child.

Roland shook his head. "Uh-unh, I said I'm not al*low*ed to tell."

Karen smiled, hanging on. "I guess there is a difference, isn't there?"

"But I'm gonna tell you anyway," Roland said. "I don't think it's fair you living like this, not knowing."

Marta was coming, Gretchen tagging along.

Karen was aware of another strange feeling, enjoying the suspense, waiting to learn something, wanting to make the feeling last, afraid the revelation would be something she already knew, or suspected. But right now an interesting, close-to-unbelievable situation, entertaining this backcountry gangster, who sat with his cowboy hat tilted low and his long legs stretched out comfortably as the maid served cocktail-hour vodka and tonic.

You can handle it, Karen thought. And you can handle Roland. Mr. Crowe. Out of a minstrel show.

She had handled—up to a point—someone much more potentially dangerous than this guy who worked for Ed Grossi but seemed to be venturing out on his own. Roland wanted something, that was obvious. Playing a nice-guy role that was about as subtle as his electric-blue suit.

Marta left them.

Roland was leaning forward playing with Gretchen on the ground, saying, "Yeah, you're a nice little Gretchie. You're a nice little Gretchie, ain'tcha, huh? Ain'tcha?"

"What is it you're going to tell me?" Karen said.

"Hey, Gretchie, come on, Gretchie, don't bite me, you little dickens. That ain't nice to bite people."

Karen decided to wait.

Roland looked up at her, his hands still fondling the dog. "You're not allowed to see anybody, what it is. I mean any man that might have serious or sexu'l intentions."

"I beg your pardon," Karen said.

"I'm supposed to keep 'em away from you. Any man believed to be serious—you know, not the grocery boy or something—I tell him to keep moving."

"Protecting the widow," Karen said. "That's what I

was afraid of. I guess I'll have to have a talk with Mr. Grossi."

"Well, there's a little more to it."

"This is Ed Grossi's idea, isn't it?"

"No, it's your husband's idea."

"My husband's?"

"He left word, no man gets near you in a serious way or as a one-nighter just fooling around or anything like it as long as you live. In other words your husband's cut off your action."

Karen was frowning. "Are you serious?"

"It's what they tell me," Roland said. "I'm the one supposed to keep 'em away from you."

"Wait a minute," Karen said, "Frank?—" Staring at Roland, but going back in her mind—hearing it again, threatening Frank, angry, yes, but the threat less than half serious—and Frank saying in a weary voice, "Karen, Karen, Karen—" The man who could write a book on paying people back. Thinking she knew him, but, good God, not taking the time to understand exactly how literal the man was. He had allowed her to think she was an equal, wife to husband. He had allowed her to ask blunt questions and finally threaten him with her independence. And he had quietly locked her up for good.

"Keep the woman in the house where she belongs."

"What?" Roland said.

"You're not kidding, are you?" Like coming out of shock, beginning to see things clearly again.

Roland seemed surprised. "No, I'm not kidding."

"Something you dreamed up."

"It's been going on, ain't it?"

"Yes, but—what do you say to them? How do you let them know?"

"You mean the guys? We tell them you don't want to see them no more."

"And what do they say?"

"Nothing."

"I mean don't they want to know why?"

"I 'magine they get the point pretty quick."

"Do you threaten them?"

"Well, there's different ways. You put the boy against the wall and tell him something, he sees you mean it." Roland grinned. "I made a point with a boy today, didn't believe at first I was serious."

"What did you do?"

"Threw him in a swimming pool."

"You don't . . . beat them up or anything like that?"

"Whatever it takes," Roland said. "That's how Ed says handle it. See, he respects your husband's wish here. But he don't want to do it himself. Fact, all he wants to know it's in somebody's hands and being taken care of."

"I'll see Ed tomorrow," Karen said.

"You sure you want to do that?"

"We're going to quit playing games, I'm sure of that."

"Well, as I see it, the one you'd have to talk to'd be Frank," Roland said. "He's the only one can call it off. Ed, he's respecting the wish of his dead buddy. You know how them people are. He can't change nothing, it's the code, or some bullshit like that." Roland was feeling more relaxed, into it now. He liked the way the woman was hanging on his words. "But you go to Ed, tell what you know, then he's liable to take me off the job and put somebody else on ain't as sympathetic. You follow me?"

"I'm not sure. Why are you . . . sympathetic?"

"I'm not one of *them,* as you can see. I work for them, but I don't think the way they do. It's like you're a white woman got mixed up with these people, I come along—I didn't take none of their oaths and shit—so I can sympathize with your situation and maybe help you out."

"How?" Karen said. "Not tell if I go out with someone?"

"No, see, I'd still have to do my job. There's people watching me, too," Roland said. "But maybe I could ease up your situation some. Come around, talk to you.

Maybe, put our minds to it, we could work something out."

"I'm not sure I follow you," Karen said, following every word, watching his eyes beneath the cool-cowboy curve of the brim and knowing exactly what he was talking about.

"I mean ease up your situation." Roland said. "I 'magine you might be getting a little tense and edgy sitting around here, your husband dead, no men you're close to. These dinks you went out with evidently didn't turn you on any."

She was tense, all right, watching him gradually moving in. She said, cautiously, "How do you know that?"

"It's my business to know. See, me and you are much closer than you realize. We got a lot in common."

"We do?" Karen said.

"See, I been thinking," Roland said. "Why would a deceased husband want to cut off his wife's . . . activity, let's say, less he was good and sore on account of she was messing around while he was alive." Roland gave Karen a friendly wink. "Just wanting to have a little fun. What's wrong with that? It's the way we're made, we got to keep active or we dry up, can't even spit."

"That's quite an assumption," Karen said. "I mean that I was cheating on my husband."

"Nobody's asking you to admit nothing you don't want to," Roland said. "It's between me and you and the bed. I mean the bedpost."

"Actually Frank had no reason—" Karen began, and stopped. Why was she trying to explain?

"It's none of my business either way," Roland said. "You don't have to confess nothing to me, lady, to be born again. That's the way I look at this setup, like a new beginning. Here you are stuck here, starting to dry up. Here I am full of notions going to waste, shit, working for them guineas. It's like, I won't tell if you won't. You scratch mine and I'll scratch yours and we'll get something cooking here—see, once you give it some thought, realize how your dead husband and his buddy've got your knees tied together and there's nothing you can do about it less I help you. You follow me? I'm giving you your big chance, lady, and it's the only one you got."

"I said to her, 'Are you all right?' She didn't answer me," Marta said. "She went to the telephone and began to speak to Mr. Grossi."

"You could hear it?" Jesus Diaz, her brother, asked.

It was dark now. They were in the street in front of the house on Isla Bahía, standing by Jesus' car, Jesus holding the cassette tape she had given him.

"I could hear it because she was making her words very clear, not in a loud voice but with force, saying, 'I don't want to see him here again. Keep that animal away from here.' Then saying, 'Why didn't you tell me yourself? I have to learn it from someone like him.' Then listening to Mr. Grossi for a long time. Then saying again, 'Keep him away from here.' But she didn't tell him everything," Marta said.

"What didn't she tell him?"

"Your friend Roland said he wanted to help her in the situation, do something for her to relieve her being tense. But she didn't mention this to Mr. Grossi—I don't know why—only that she didn't want to see Roland again. Very disturbed, but cold in the way she said it, not screaming or shouting. I thought of the time she came home with her car smashed in front and Mister came home with his same car smashed in the side."

Jesus said, "All of that with Mr. Grossi is on this tape?"

"Yes, of course. Every phone conversation today."

"I give it to Roland, he'll hear it," Jesus said. "He'll know she told Mr. Grossi."

"Then don't give it to him," Marta said.

"You crazy?" Jesus said.

Roland heard about it the same evening, in Vivian Arzola's office. Vivian telling him he was lucky Ed Grossi had already gone home. Roland looking out the thirty-ninth floor window at all that night glitter over the Beach.

"Why?" Roland said.

"Because maybe this time he would have killed you he was so angry."

Roland said, "Lady, I'm the boy didn't testify in court against somebody, and went to Butler. You remember? I just got *back* yesterday. He puts me on a job, I do it the way I see fit to. Does he want another boy? That's up to him. But don't start talking about him doing me harm. There's an old Cuban saying, you fuck with the bull, you get a horn in the ass."

"Where'd you get that suit?" Vivian said.

Roland grinned. "You like it?"

"It's the worst looking suit I ever saw."

"That's my sweet girl," Roland said, coming away from the window to put a leg up on the edge of Vivian's desk, "your old self again. What else he say?"

"He's going to tell you himself. Keep away from Mrs. DiCilia."

"But not taking me off it."

"Do what you're told. Nothing more."

"You listen in and hear her talking to him?"

"It's recorded here," Vivian said. "I can listen if I want. You try to lie to him, he'll play it for you."

"I got nothing to hide. I told her her old man set up the deal, that's all. So everybody understands each other. I asked her if there was anything I could do for her."

"I can hear you," Vivian said, "the way you'd say it. Did she scream for help?"

"She was nice about the whole thing. What I'm surprised at, she went and called Ed."

"Well, stay away from her, that's all."

"Sure, that's how he wants it. What I better have, though, are all the back tapes. You think I come to see you, it's the tapes I need most."

"Why?" Vivian said.

"You want me to do the job or not?"

Vivian, sitting at her desk, studied him, trying to catch a glimpse of how his mind was working.

"See, now the woman knows she's being watched, she's gonna be more careful," Roland said.

"Thanks to you."

"No, it's better this way, let her know where she stands. But I got to listen to the back tapes. See, get to recognize voices if any of 'em call again and don't use names. You understand?"

"I understand that," Vivian said, "but I think I better talk to Ed first. He'll be back in a few days."

"He went out of town?"

"He'll be back."

"Meanwhile," Roland said, "we're sitting here humping the dog, huh? What I could do is return 'em before he gets back. Otherwise, something happens, Ed sees the work wasn't done properly, he looks around for who's to blame and, like that, you're back in your overalls picking oranges."

Roland walked out with a cardboard box full of cassette tapes. Fucking Cubans, he hadn't met one yet you couldn't hold their job over 'em like a club and get whatever you wanted.

6.

If porpoise were really so smart, Maguire would think, how come they put up with all this shit?

The porpoise could ask Maguire the same question. Or Lolly the sea lion.

In the cement-block room off the show pool, Maguire and Lolly would look at each other. Maguire holding the mike to announce Brad Allen and the World-Famous Seascape Porpoise and Sea Lion Show. Lolly waiting to go on, the opening act. Maguire wondering if Lolly ever played with her beachball when no one was around. Lolly wondering—what? Looking at him with her sad eyes.

Maguire would announce the show, hearing his voice outside on the P.A. system as he looked through the crack in the door at the people in the grandstand.

"And now . . . here's Brad!"

After the show Brad Allen would say to Maguire, "Look, how many times? You don't say, 'Here's Brad,' for Christ sake. You ever watch Johnny Carson, the way they do it? You say, 'And now . . . heeeeeeeeeeere's Brad!' "

"I don't know why, but I have trouble with that," Maguire would say.

Brad Allen was show director, star, working manager of:

SEASCAPE
PORPOISE SHOW

SHARKS * SEA LIONS

S.E. Seventeenth Street Causeway
At Port Everglades

TURN HERE!

He would say to Maguire, "Are you stupid or something? I don't think it's that hard, do you?"

"No, it isn't," Maguire would say.

"I believe you're supposed to be experienced—"

"The thing is, down at Marathon we didn't have the same kind of show," Maguire would try to explain. "I mean it wasn't quite as, you know, showy."

"Down there, did you know the names of the dolphin?" Brad always got onto that. "Could you identify each one by name?"

"Yeah, I knew their names."

"Then how come you don't know them here?"

"I know them. There's Pepper, Dixie, Penny, Bonzai—"

"Robyn says yesterday you were trying to get Penny to do a tailwalk. Penny doesn't do the tailwalk, Pebbles does the tailwalk."

"I get those two mixed up."

"The other day you thought Bonnie was Yvonne. Bonnie's got the scar from the shark—"

"Right."

"—and Yvonne's at least two hundred pounds heavier, ten feet long, you can't tell them apart. Work on it, okay? Take Robyn over the tank with you and see if you can name them for her. Then come back to the show pool and do the same thing. Is that too much to ask?"

Or, Brad Allen would say:

"The Flying Dolphin Show, you keep leaving out the Mopey Dick part."

"I forget."

"He lays up on the ledge on his side, doesn't move a muscle. Wait for the laughs. Then you say, 'And that's' pause 'why we call him *Mopey* Dick.' "

"I'll try to remember," Maguire would say.

Five months of it, January through May.

Brad Allen waiting for him when he first walked in, pale, a Wayne-County-Jail pallor, carrying his lined raincoat and suitcase, right off the Delta flight. Brad Allen glancing at a letter the Seascape Management Company had sent him, holding the sheet of paper like it was stained or smelled bad.

"It says you've had experience."

"A year at Marathon," Maguire had said, adding on five months.

"What've you been doing since?"

"Well, traveling and working mostly," Maguire had said. "Colorado, I worked for the Aspen Ski Corporation, also at the Paragon Ballroom. I worked at an airport, a zoo, a TV station. I was the weatherman. I tended bar different places. Let's see, I was an antique dealer. Yeah, and I worked a job at a country club."

"Well, this is no country club," Brad Allen had said. The serious tone, making it sound hard because he had to hire the guy. "How old are you?"

"Thirty," Maguire had said, subtracting six years—after walking in and seeing how young the help was. Like summer-camp counselors in their sneakers and white shorts, red T-shirts with a flying-porpoise decal and SEASCAPE lettered in white. (Brad Allen wore white shorts and a red-trimmed white T-shirt with the porpoise and SEASCAPE in red. He also wore a white jacket and red warmups and sometimes a red, white, and blue outfit.)

"How long you been thirty?"

What was Brad Allen? Maybe thirty-two, thirty-three. The guy staring at Maguire, suspicious, wanting to catch him in a lie. For what?

"What difference does it make?" Maguire had said. "I'm an out-going person, I like to be with people, I don't mind working hard and"—laying on a little extra—"I'm always willing to learn if there's something I don't know."

It took him a few days to get used to the white shorts and the red T-shirt—thinking about what Andre Patterson would say if he saw the outfit; like, man, you real cute. Within two months Maguire was as brown as the rest of them, and his sneakers were beginning to show some character. He did believe he could pass for thirty. Why not? He felt younger than that. He was out in the sunshine. The work was clean, not too hard. He was eating a lot of fruit. Smoking a little grass now and then with Lesley. Not drinking too much. The pay was terrible, two-sixty a week, but he was getting by. Living in a one-room efficiency at an Old-Florida-looking stucco place called The Casa Loma, fifty bucks a week, next door to Lesley who lived in the manager's apartment with her Aunt Leona. What else? Air-conditioned, two blocks from the ocean—

The people he worked with—R.D. Hooker, Chuck, Robyn and Lesley—reminded him of high school.

Hooker, a strong, curly-haired Florida boy, twenty-three years old. A clean liver, dedicated. Hooker would go down into the eighteen-foot tank, Neptune's Realm, with a face mask and air hose and play with the porpoise even when he didn't have to, *between* shows. One time Hooker said to Chuck, the custodian-trainee, "I don't know what's wrong with Bonnie today. First she won't let me touch her, then she butts me. Then she comes up and starts yanking on my goddarn air hose like to pull it out of my mouth. Knowing what she was doing."

Chuck listened to every word and said, "Yeah? How come she was doing that?"

Maguire said, "It sounds like she's getting her period."

Hooker said, "What's it got to do with her acting nasty?"

Maguire would listen to them talk, amazed, nobody putting anybody on or down. Maguire said, "R.D., you ever talk to them? I mean understand them?"

"Sometimes," Hooker said. "Like I'm getting so I can understand Penny when I ask her a question?"

"No shit," Maguire said. "What do you ask her?"

"Oh, feeding her I might say, 'You like that, huh? Isn't that good?' "

"And what does she say?"

"She goes like—" Hooker did something with the inside of his mouth and made a clickity-click, kitty-cat, Donald Duck sound.

"Oh," Maguire said.

Hooker came on his day off and worked with the two young dolphins in the training tank, hunkered down on the boards for hours, talking to them gently and showing them his hands. Dedicated.

Chuck was on his way to becoming dedicated. He personally wrote two hundred post cards to Star-Kist Tuna, Bumble Bee, VanCamp, Ralston Purina, and H.J. Heinz, telling them to quit murdering dolphin or he would never eat their products again.

Robyn was dedicated, though didn't appear to be. She was a serious girl and didn't smile much or seem to be listening when you said something to her. Unless it was Brad Allen who said it. Brad Allen could tell Robyn to dive down to the bottom of the show pool with Dixie, shoot up over the twelve-foot bar and do a tailwalk across the pool, and Robyn would try it. When Brad Allen told her she was doing a good job, Robyn became squirmy and maybe wet her white shorts a little. Nice tight shorts—

Though not as tight or short as Lesley's. Lesley's showed a little cheek. She never pulled at them though, the way Robyn did when she got squirmy. What Lesley got was pouty. She'd put on her hurt look and say, "It's not my turn to feed the sharks, it's hers. If you think I'm going in there every day you're out of your fucking mind." Lesley was dedicated, but not to nurse sharks. She didn't think it was funny when she was standing hip deep in the pool trying to feed a hunk of bluerunner to a shark, and Maguire, on the platform above, would say to the crowd, "Let's give Lesley a nice hand"—pause—"she may need one some day."

Lesley had a pile of wavy brown hair she combed several times an hour. One night, during Maguire's fourth month, Lesley said to him, "I think I'm falling in love with you." She looked so good lying there in the dim light with her hair and her white breasts exposed, Maguire almost said he loved her, too. But he didn't.

Brad Allen was *very* dedicated. Brad Allen was also serious and tiresome. He made Maguire tired. Maguire wondered why Brad Allen didn't get tired of being Brad Allen. Once, Maguire took a couple of puffs on a joint before announcing the show and said, over the P.A. system, "Heeeeeeeeeeeeeeeeeeeeeeeeeeeeeeeeeer's Brad," holding the "here's" almost as long as he could. And after the show Brad Allen said to him, "Now that's a little better."

Seascape, the layout, reminded Maguire of a small tropical World's Fair; round white buildings, striped awnings, and blue and yellow pennants among shrubs and royal palms.

There was Neptune's Realm you could walk into and look through windows to watch the porpoise and sea creatures glide past, underwater. Topside they put on the Flying Dolphin Show.

There was Shark Lagoon, a pool full of brown nurse sharks and a few giant sea turtles.

There was the Porpoise Petting Pool, where you could touch Misty and Gippy's hard-boiled-egg skin and feed them minnows, three-for-a-quarter.

At the Grandstand Arena Brad Allen put on the main event, the World-Famous Seascape Porpoise and Sea Lion Show: "where these super-smart mammals perform their aquatic acrobatics."

Back in the Alligator Pit a Seminole Indian used to wrestle twelve-foot gators, but the Seminole quit and went to Disney World, and R.D. Hooker only tried it a couple of times; so the alligators and a crocodile were there if you wanted to look at them.

Yellow- and white-striped awnings covered the refreshment stand and gift shop. A fifty-cent Sky Ride in two-seater gondolas gave you a low aerial view of the grounds, the tanks and pools of blue water, the white cement walks and buildings among the imported palm trees: a clean, manicured world just off the S.E. 17th Street Causeway.

"If you don't like it, why don't you quit?" Lesley said, getting a little pouty.

"I didn't say I didn't like it, I said it wasn't *real,*" Maguire said, Maguire driving Lesley's yellow Honda, heading home to the Casa Loma. "It's like a refuge. Nothing can happen to you there, you're safe. But it's got nothing to do with reality. It's like you're given security, but in exchange for it you have to give up your*self*. You have to become somebody else.

Lesley said, "Jesus, what's safe about getting down in the water, feeding those fucking sharks? I've done it every day this week, you know it? Robyn's off probably giving Brad some head."

Maguire said, "Come on, the sharks feed all night. You jiggle a piece of fish, it's for the tourists. I'm not talking about that kind of being safe. I mean *here,* you live in a little world that's got nothing to do with the real world. You're sheltered—"

"I'm sheltered?"

"We are, working there. What's a really big problem? Misty eats some popcorn, gets constipated. Pebbles is grouchy, won't imitate the Beatles. Everybody's going, 'Christ, what's the matter with Pebbles?' Spend *months,* maybe a year training a dolphin to jump through a hoop, come up seventeen feet in the air and ring the school bell."

Lesley said, "Yeah?" She still didn't get it.

"They're doing something that dolphins don't normally do, right?"

Lesley thought a moment. "Yeah—but they jump. Out in the wild they jump all the time."

"They shoot baskets? They bowl out there?"

"It's to show how intelligent they are," Lesley said, "how they can be trained."

"Here's the point," Maguire said, wishing the Honda

was air-conditioned, wishing the lady in front of him would turn, for Christ sake, if she was going to turn, *turn*. "They don't normally, the dolphin, they don't pretend they're playing baseball out in the ocean or jump up and take a piece of fish out of somebody's mouth, right?"

"If you don't like it," Lesley said, "what do you do it for?"

Jesus, Maguire thought. He said, "Just follow the point I want to make, okay? I'm not saying I don't like it. I'm only saying it's like playing make-believe. The dolphin wouldn't be here, they wouldn't be doing the tricks if we didn't teach them. You see what I mean? They'd be out there doing something else, we'd be doing something else. But no, we made this up. The dolphins and us, we're playing with ourselves. We're going through the motions of something that doesn't have anything to do with reality."

"So?"

Oh, Christ. "So—if they're not real dolphins doing all that kind of shit, what're we? Reciting the canned humor, throwing them pieces of codfish—what're we?"

"I was a waitress, a place on Las Olas," Lesley said. "That was real, real shit. You like to ask me what I'd rather do?"

"I'd like to borrow your car this evening," Maguire said. "What're the chances?"

He poured himself a white rum with a splash of lemon concentrate, left the venetian blinds half closed and sat for awhile, the room looking old and worn-out in the dimness. Fifty bucks a week including black and white TV, it was still a bargain. He could hear the hi-fi going next-door, Lesley boogying around the apartment to the Bee-Gees, ignoring her aunt, who was a little deaf. A nice woman, Maguire would sit and talk to her sometimes, listen to episodes from her past life in Cincinnati, Ohio, until he'd tell her he had to go to bed, wake up early. Lesley never sat and listened even for a minute. Lesley would roll her eyes when she saw an episode coming and get out of there. Lesley had no feelings for others; but she sure had a nice firm healthy little body.

Maguire showered and had another rum and lemon while he put on his good clothes. Pale beige slacks, dark-blue sportshirt and a skimpy dacron sportcoat, faded light-blue, he'd got at Burdine's for forty-five bucks. He loved the sportcoat because, for some reason, it made him think of Old Florida and made him feel like a native. (A Maguire dictum: wherever you are, fit in, look like you belong. In Colorado wear a sheepskin coat and lace-up boots.) He got the *Detroit Free Press* clipping out of the top drawer, from under his sweat socks, and slipped it into the inside coat pocket. He then went next door and asked Lesley's aunt if he could use the phone; he'd be sure to get the charges and pay for it.

He said to Lesley, "You want to turn that down a little?"

Lesley said, "Who're you calling, your hot date?"

"I don't have a hot date."

"I thought you were going out."

"Turn the music down, okay?"

Maguire gave the operator the Detroit number and waited. He felt nervous. He wished Lesley would quit watching him.

"Aren't you gonna clean up?"

"You want me to leave, say so."

"I get back, I'll take you out to dinner."

In the phone, Andre Patterson's wife said, "Hello?"

"Okay?" Maguire said to Lesley. "Go on, get cleaned up." Then into the phone:

"Hi, this is Cal Maguire. How you doing?" He had to listen while Andre's wife told him she was piss-poor, if he really wanted to know about it, having trouble getting her ADC checks, had her phone disconnected for a while. Maguire said yeah, he'd been trying to get hold of her, calling information. He said, "Listen, you know the deal at the club? . . . The country club, Andre and I and Grover. I asked you the man's name? Remember?

. . . No, I've got it. What I was wondering, you know, Andre said the man was paying them back for something? At the club, something happened there to the man. I wondered if Andre ever spoke to you about it . . . If he mentioned to you what it was happened out there. Like maybe the man's wife was involved, you know, maybe she was insulted or something and that's what got the man upset." Christ, upset—willing to pay them forty-five hundred to go out there and hit the place. "Uh-huh, yeah, that's right . . . But he never said anything about the man's wife, huh? . . . No, I was just wondering. Hey, well listen, tell Andre I'm gonna write to him, okay? . . . Fine, I'll be talking to you." Shit.

"Very mysterious," Lesley said, holding a beach towel wrapped around her. "Who's Andre?"

"Friend of mine."

"What'd somebody get upset about?"

Maguire said, "I know it's your aunt's phone and you're letting me use you car and all, but how about if you keep your nose out of my personal business, okay?"

"Yeah," Lesley said, "well, how about if you keep your ass out of my car, you want to get snotty about it."

"You're a beauty," Maguire said. "You got the maturity of about a five-year-old."

"Keep thinking it," Lesley said, "walking to work every day." She turned, letting the towel come open, giving him a flash as she went into the bedroom.

There you are, Maguire thought, walking up the street toward A1A. The kind of question you'd climb all the way up the mountain to ask the old man sitting there in his loincloth.

In the light of eternity, is it better to sell out and ride or stand up and walk?

And the old man would look at him with his calm, level gaze and say—

He'd say—

Maguire was still trying to think of an answer, standing on the oceanfront corner, when the girl visiting from Mitchell, Indiana, picked him up, said, "Heck, it's nothing," and went out of her way to drop him off at Harbor Beach Parkway.

7.

An appraiser friend of Maguire's, a guy who bought and sold pretty much out of his backdoor, once said to him, "You walk out with a color TV, you realize the mirror hanging on the wall there, gilded walnut, might be a George II? Early eighteenth century, man, worth at least three grand." Maguire went to the library, looked through art books, made notes and lifted a copy of *Kovel's Complete Antiques Price List* from the reference shelf. In his work—during the short periods he was into B and E, usually to pick up some traveling money—he'd come across a few antiques and art objects of value.

But nothing like the display in Mrs. DiCilia's sitting room. He was looking at a Queen Anne desk—four drawers, stubby little pedestal legs, worth at least four grand—when the maid came in again, a dog following her, and told him to please be seated, Missus would come to him very soon. A sharp-looking Cuban girl, nice accent. Maguire said thank you and then, as the maid was leaving, "How you doing?"

Marta stopped. She said, "Yes?"

"How's it going? You like it here?" Always friendly to the help. "I think it'd be a nice place to work."

Marta, still surprised: "Yes, it is."

"But I wouldn't want to have to dust all this," Maguire said.

The maid left, but the little gray and white dog remained, watching Maguire apprehensively, ready to bark or run.

"Relax," Maguire said to the dog and continued looking around the sitting room.

Bird cage table, not bad. Worth about seven and a half.

Pair of slipseat Chippendale chairs in walnut. Now we're getting there. Seventy-five hundred, maybe eight grand.

Hummel figurines, if you liked Hummel. Fifty bucks each. A couple that might go as high as a hundred and a quarter.

Plates—very impressive. Stevenson, Enoch Wood's shell-border pattern. Six, seven thousand bucks worth of plates on one shelf.

And *yes,* Peachblow vases, the real thing. Creamy red-rose and yellow. Jesus, with the gargoyle stand. Name your price.

A picture of Pope Pius XII. The Last Supper. And some real paintings, old forests and misty green mountains, a signed Durand, an Alvan Fisher, nineteenth-century Hudson River school. A few others he didn't recognize—sitting down now as he studied the painting—

And jumping up quickly to look at the chair—Jesus, feeling the turnings of the arms. Louis XVI bergère, in walnut. Pretty sure it was a real one.

He sat in the chair again, carefully, and began thinking about the woman who lived here and owned this collection. Before, he had pictured a dumpy sixty-year-old Italian woman in the kitchen, rolling dough, making tomato paste, a woman with an accent. He'd lay it out to her: Your husband owes us money. She'd pay or she wouldn't, and he could forget about it.

But if she knew antiques—maybe he could fake it a little, establish some kind of rapport, trust . . . confidence?

The dog came over and began sniffing.

"That's fish," Maguire said. He didn't stoop to pet the dog or say anything else.

Karen, in the doorway, saw this much. And the color of his pants and shirt beneath the jacket, making her hesitate a moment.

"Mr. Maguire?"

He looked up to see a slim, good-looking woman in beige slacks, a dark-blue shirt with white buttons, hand extended.

Maguire rose, giving her a pleasant smile, shaking his head a little. They shook hands politely and he said, seriously then, "You know something?"

Karen expected him to say, I've heard a lot about you, Mrs. DiCilia. Something along that line.

But he didn't. He said, "We've got matching outfits on. Tan and blue."

Karen said, "You suppose it means something?" Playing it as straight as he was.

"I don't know about you," Maguire said, "but I got all dressed up. This particular outfit is from Burdine's, up on Federal Highway."

"I've heard of Burdine's," Karen said, "but I'm not sure I've heard of you. You were a friend of my husband's?"

"Well, we weren't exactly close. I worked for him once."

Karen said, "And you want to know if I'm all right? If I need anything? What else? Are you with Roland or on your own?"

"I don't know anybody named Roland," Maguire said.

"So you're an independent. All right," Karen said, "let's go out on the patio. That's where we hold the squeeze sessions."

"The what?"

"Come on, I'm anxious to hear your pitch." She walked past him to the French doors.

It had felt like a good start. But now, she wasn't being cool, she was ice-cold, assuming way too much. Maguire hesitated. He said, "You've got some very nice pieces here. The bergère, is it authentic Louis Seize?"

Now Karen paused at the doors to look back and seemed to study him a moment.

"The what?"

Maguire grinned. Was she kidding? She waited, looking at him, and he wasn't sure.

"The chair. If it's real, it belongs in a museum."

"It *is* in a museum," Karen said. She turned and walked through the doors.

Putting him on, Maguire decided. Not wanting to sound agreeable or give him anything. He followed her out to the patio, where a torch was burning and swimming pool lights reflected in the clear water, Maguire looking around, thinking, So this is what it's like. Sit out here at night, watch the running lights, the powerboats going by on the Intercoastal.

Ring for the maid, get her with some mysterious signal, because there she was. Maguire said rum would be fine, surprised, wondering why Mrs. DiCilia was being sociable, hearing her ask for a martini with ice. Put that down: not "on the rocks" but "with ice." Yes, very nice; sit out here on the patio of your Spanish-Moorish million-dollar home that was full of antiques and art objects and—what?

He was going to say he was sorry for coming so late, or early—one or the other—and hoped he wasn't inconveniencing her. But why? Why suck around?

He said, "Besides all this, what's it like to be rich?"

Karen didn't say anything.

"Never mind," Maguire said. "It doesn't matter."

"I was thinking," Karen said. "If you really want to know, it's boring. I guess it doesn't have to be, but it is."

"I don't follow you."

"You asked me, I told you, it's boring," Karen said. "Next question. Let's get to the point, all right?"

The dog was sniffing around his foot again. Maguire crossed his leg.

Mrs. DiCilia was on the muscle, a little edgy, yes; because she was waiting for him to pull some kind of scam. Out here for the squeeze session: probably one of a long line of guys who'd come to make a pitch, take advantage of the poor widow. The slim, good-looking great-looking widow. Maguire resented her assumption, being put in that category, somebody out to con her. The lady sitting there waiting for the pitch.

The goddamn dog pawing his knee, scratching the material. Maguire reached down with one hand and moved the dog aside.

Karen watched him.

Sitting back he took the newspaper clipping out of his pocket, unfolded it carefully and handed it to her.

Karen said, "What is it?" In the soft glow of torch-light she could only read the headline. ARMED TRIO ROBS COUNTRY CLUB.

"That was myself and two associates," Maguire said. "Your husband offered to pay us fifteen hundred each to go in and hit the place. Make them look dumb or give it some bad publicity, I don't know. We did the job, but we never got paid."

Karen said, "Deep Run Country Club, Bloomfield Hills."

"That's the one."

"It happened when, last August?"

"Right. The sixteenth."

"We visited Detroit in August—no, it was July," Karen said. "Frank played golf there a few times as a guest. He liked the club, so he applied for a membership."

"And they turned him down," Maguire said. Karen nodded. "I thought maybe you'd been insulted out there. You know, something personal."

"What do you think Frank DiCilia being turned down is, if it isn't an insult?"

"Yeah, I guess so. But how come if you were living here at the time?—"

"Why can't he have a membership in Detroit? That's what it's like to be rich," Karen said. "So what is it you want, fifteen hundred dollars?"

"Each, for the three of us. The other two guys were convicted. They're in Jackson, but I'll see they get theirs."

"You got off?" She seemed interested.

"It's a long story, and if you're already bored—" Maguire said.

Karen said, "That's all you want?"

"That's all we got coming."

"You could've said . . . ten thousand."

"And you could've known about the deal," Maguire said, "depending on what you and your hubby talked about. It was a straight fifteen hundred apiece, no sick pay or retirement benefits."

Now, yes or no? Waiting for her to make up her mind. She didn't seem as edgy. She said let's have another drink and that surprised him. The maid appeared and left, and when she appeared again Karen was asking him if he lived in Florida or was he visiting.

He told her he worked at Seascape. "You know, the porpoise show? Practically around the corner from here."

"I've passed it," Karen said. "You really work there?" Sounding interested and a little surprised. "Get the porpoise to jump through hoops, that kind of thing?"

"We get 'em to do everything but mate in midair," Maguire said.

"They won't do that for you?"

"I think they go to a motel. Five months, I've never seen one of 'em even, well, get aroused."

Now she was studying him and didn't say anything for a moment.

"Amazing."

"Well, I wouldn't like it either," Maguire said. "People watching."

"No, I mean that you work there," Karen said. "And you seem to know antiques—What else do you do?"

"Rob country clubs," Maguire said, "and have a hard time collecting. I'm enjoying the drink and the chat, but just for my peace of mind, are you gonna honor your husband's obligation or what?"

Karen said, *"Honor* his obligation—" and seemed amused now. "Is that what it is, honoring his obligation?"

"You can call it whatever you want," Maguire said, "as long as we're both talking about the same deal."

"Do you do this sort of thing often?"

"What sort of thing?"

"Rob country clubs?"

"That was the first time."

"But you've robbed other places."

He didn't say anything.

"Do you carry a gun?"

"Why?"

"I'm curious, that's all."

"Do you fool around?" Maguire said.

"What?"

"Do you pick up guys, take 'em to bed? Or you just ask a lot of questions about their personal life?"

"I believe you came to me," Karen said. "You're the one that wants something."

"And if I'm not polite and answer your questions I can go fuck myself, huh?"

Karen didn't say anything. She got up, walked from the patio to the house and in through the French doors.

Maguire waited. Shit. Thinking again of the old man sitting on top of the mountain in his loincloth.

In the light of eternity, is it better to take a bunch of shit with the hope of getting paid, or—

Karen came back to the patio carrying something in each hand, something wrapped in white tissue paper and, in the hand she extended to him, a packet of bills. He couldn't believe it. New one hundred dollar bills. They were sticking together, only about an inch of them, they were so new.

"Forty-five hundred dollars," Karen said.

Maguire thinking, the first thing in his mind: There's more. Right in the house.

"Can I ask you one more question?"

"Go ahead," Maguire said, putting the money in his inside coat pocket. He could feel it against his ribs.

She pulled her chair closer to his and sat down before extending the tissue-wrapped package.

"What is it?"

She watched him, but didn't say anything.

Taking it then, feeling the weight, he knew what it was. Maguire unwrapped enough of the tissue paper to see the gun, wrapped it together again and handed it back to her.

She said, "Do you know what it is, the make?"

"It's a Beretta nine-millimeter Parabellum, holds eight rounds in the clip. How much you pay for it?"

"I didn't buy it. It was my husband's."

"You could get something like four hundred for it on the street."

"I don't want to sell it," Karen said, "I want to know how to use it."

"For what?"

"Protection."

"It isn't a good idea," Maguire said. "People who don't own guns don't get shot as much as people who do."

"Will you show me how it works?"

"If I don't, what? You want the money back?"

"The money's yours. You've already earned that." She waited.

"It's got a little crossbolt safety above the trigger. You push it to off, slide the top back and forward again and you're ready to go," Maguire said. "Which is what I'm gonna do if it's okay. Take my money and run."

"You're very direct," Karen said, and seemed to be studying him again. "You admit some things and then you stop."

"It's not that I have anything to hide," Maguire said, "it's the feeling I'm on the carpet, being questioned."

She said, "I'm sorry, I really am." There was a silence, but she continued to look at him.

Maguire said, "That's okay. I guess—as you say, I

walk in here, give you a story, why should you believe me?"

"I do though," Karen said. She seemed to smile then. "Will you tell me something else?"

"Probably," Maguire said.

"What's the difference between a porpoise and a dolphin?"

Maguire found a note on his pillow that said, in a forward-slanting Magic Marker scrawl, "Knock if you are not mad!!!"

He reached across the bed to the wall—to a fading garden at Versailles, green-on-yellow wallpaper—and rapped on it three times.

Lesley came in wearing a short see-through nighty and several rollers in her hair, head somewhat lowered to gaze up at Maguire with a practiced, hurt-little-girl expression.

"I thought you were gonna take me out to dinner."

"I must've got mixed up, who was mad at who," Maguire said. "I had something over on the beach."

"I *was* mad," Lesley said, "but I'm not anymore."

"How come?"

"You didn't have to talk to me like that."

"Did you go out?"

"No"—pouting—"I sat there with Aunt Leona watching TV all night."

Poor little thing—he was supposed to comfort her, tell her he was sorry. He wasn't annoyed or upset. In fact, he didn't feel much of anything toward Lesley, one way or the other. He was catching glimpses of Karen DiCilia in the glow of the torch, part of her face in shadow, the light reflecting on her dark hair. Dark but not Italian-dark, the woman not anything like he'd imagined the wife of Frank DiCilia.

Lesley said, "Are you going to bed or you gonna read?"

It was strange, in that moment he did feel a little sorry for her, standing there in her see-through nighty and her curlers. He said, "It's late. Might as well go to bed."

"You want me to get in with you?"

"You bet," Maguire said, getting undressed as she turned off the light and pulled back the green and yellow spread.

"There," Lesley said. "God, isn't it good?"

"It sure is."

"Shit, I forgot my curlers."

She sat up, took out the ones in back and got down there again.

"Ouuuu, that hurts. But it's okay. Now it's okay. Ouuuuu, is it ever." After awhile she said, "Cal?"

"What?"

"If my aunt knew we did this? She'd shit. You know it?"

"I guess," Maguire said.

"We're watching TV? She goes on and on about in Cincinnati she's at a picnic with this guy named Herman or Henry or something and how he grabbed her and kissed her. God, it was like it freaked her out, and she was *my* age. In the guy's car. I want to say to her, 'Aunt Leona, you ever go down on him?' She'd actually shit, you know it?"

"I bet," Maguire said.

"No, she was twenty-*three*. It was just before she got married. But not to Herman. My uncle's name was Thomas. That's what they called him all the time, Thomas. I can't imagine them doing it. Can you imagine Aunt Leona doing it?"

"No," Maguire said.

"She's in there snoring away, all this beauty cream on. You should see her."

He didn't say anything.

"Well, I better get my ass beddy-by. I'll see you in the morning."

"Night," Maguire said.

"Don't play with it too much," Lesley said.

"I won't."

The door closed.

He could see Karen DiCilia in shadow and firelight, the clean-shining dark hair, features composed. Karen DiCilia, Karen something else, Karen Hill originally. He'd found out a few things. If she could ask questions he could, too. And then she had asked a few more. Calvin, is it? Yeah. Calvin doesn't go with Maguire. It should be Al instead of Cal, Aloysius Maguire, a good mick name. Well, Karen doesn't go too well with DiCilia, does it? And the good-looking woman saying, No, it should never have gone with DiCilia.

Sometimes we're bored, willing to try something new and different. Change for the sake of change.

Maguire saying, Right.

Sometimes, then, we're too impulsive, we make up our minds too quickly.

True.

Sometimes we talk too much, say things we don't mean.

Very true. (Talking, but what was she *saying*?)

And we get into a bind, a situation that offers few if any options and then we're stuck and we don't know what to do.

Maguire saying, Uh-huh.

Maguire almost saying, If you want to tell me what you're stuck in, what the problem is, why don't you, instead of beating around?

Almost, but not saying it. Because what if she told him? And expected him to help her out in some way; man, with the kind of people who'd been associated with her husband and were probably still hanging around—Then what, chickenfat, sit there and grin at her or get involved in something that's none of your business?

This was a very good-looking woman. The kind, ordinarily, it would be a pleasure to help out and have her feel grateful. This one, he was pretty sure, could be warm and giving.

But right now she was in some kind of no-option bind and had a keen interest in firearms . . . while

Maguire had a vivid memory of the six by eight cells in the Wayne County Jail and what it was like to go to trial facing 20 to life.

So he had said, when it was his turn again, "Well listen, Karen, it's been very nice talking to you," and thanked her again and got out of there.

Lying in bed he began to think, But maybe she just needs somebody to talk to. Somebody she feels would understand her situation. Or keep the local con artists away. It didn't necessarily have to be anything heavy. What was the risk in talking to her, finding out a little more?

She was a good-looking woman.

He wondered how old she was.

He wondered how many more new one hundred dollar bills there were in her house.

8.

Arnold came from the bedroom carrying a yellow canvas bag that had a zippered flap on the side for a tennis racket. Roland was on the balcony looking over the rail, holding onto his cowboy hat due to the wind off the ocean. Arnold stared at Roland's back, at the bright-blue material pulled tight across the shoulders.

Roland turned. As he saw Arnold watching him, he said, "How's Barry?"

Arnold walked over to the coffee table and dropped the bag. "Fifty-four thousand," Arnold said.

Roland came in from the balcony. "I asked you how's Barry."

"He's in traction. He'll be in traction six months. Also his kidney and his spleen's fucked up."

"Tell him if he's gonna dive, he should do it in the deep end," Roland said. He moved past Arnold to the canvas bag and picked it up. "Wouldn't think paper'd be this heavy, would you?"

"You gonna look at it?"

"I know what it looks like," Roland said. "You're doing good, Arnie. Keep it up."

"You know I'm gonna pay you, right?"

"Sure, I do."

"Well, how about—you know, since this isn't strictly speaking a shylock deal—we make a different kind of arrangement."

"Like what, Arnie?"

"See, the way it is, I keep paying the vig, how'm I ever gonna get to the principle?"

"Beats the shit out of me," Roland said.

"You know what I mean? I didn't borrow the money. I'm only paying the man back his investment."

"Yeah? What's the difference?"

"It's *diff*erent. You got guys borrow money from you, they know going in what the vig is. But this was a business deal."

"They're all business deals," Roland said, "but vig's vig and the amount owed's something else. Didn't they teach you that at school, Arnie?"

"I tried to explain it to Ed—"

"I know you did. And he told you to talk to me," Roland said. "It's the same way, a man, a guy owns one of the biggest hotels on the strip, he borrows money, he pays the vig. Every week. He's got a problem, he comes to me with it. Man with a restaurant right here in Hallandale, shit, half a dozen appliance stores over on federal highway, picture show, bunch of motels—they all pay the vig, Arnie. They understand it's the way you do business."

"Right, shylock business, I understand that." Arnold moving around, bit his lip. "But this is *diff*erent."

"And I ask you how-so?"

"I didn't *borrow* the money, Ed in*vested* it."

"But you lost it, so you have to pay it back."

"I didn't lose it—"

Roland had his palm up, facing Arnold. "We ought to agree on something here."

"Okay, I lost it."

"Now then," Roland said, "when you come to paying back, what's the difference? Paying back is paying back, whether it's money you lost or money you borrowed. See, your losing it—we give you money, we don't ask you what you're gonna do with it, like the bank. You can flush it down the toilet if you want. Long as you pay it back."

"Okay," Arnold said, "I owe you five hundred and forty grand. I can pay you back in time, you know that. But I can't if I keep paying the fucking vig. Look, ten weeks from now, fifty-four *thousand* a week, man, where the fuck am I? I will've paid out five hundred forty grand, right? And I'm still not into the fucking principle. I'm never into it. You know what I got to do? I mean to get what I'm paying you."

"I don't know," Roland said, "ask your mommy for it?"

"I got to deal in hard shit, man, and that's a totally different business. Get into that Mexican brown, nobody even likes it, I got to keep a line coming through here and beg, im*plore,* dealers to take the shit. That's what I'm into now, myself, that's all."

"Your little friends," Roland said, "where'd they go?"

"Who knows. Fuck 'em. I said to Ed, okay, then back me again on the Colombian thing. Three times, three loads, you take my cut as well as your own, I'm paid off."

"And he said?"

"Shit, you know what he said."

Roland buttoned his suitcoat and switched the canvas bag from his right hand to his left, ready to go.

He said, "It's hard out here in the world of commerce, ain't it, Arnie?"

But rewarding to those who put their nose to the grindstone and their ear to a box-full of cassette tapes, the way Roland did for twenty-four hours and fourteen minutes spread over three days, listening to something like one hundred forty-six different cassettes.

And ninety-nine percent nothing. Somebody called the weather every day. The lady called her hairdresser once a week, this queer who scolded her and acted impatient. (What'd she take that kind of shit for?) She talked to some people in Detroit a few times; nothing. She talked to her daughter Julie in Los Angeles; listened to her daughter bitch about work and her husband fooling around, the daughter talking away, never asking how her mother was doing. ("Hang up," Roland would say to himself. "Whyn't you hang up?")

There were calls to Marta, short conversations in Spanish. Then a woman calling from the *Miami Herald* a couple of times, wanting to interview her, take some pictures of Mrs. DiCilia at home, Mrs. DiCilia saying not now, some other time.

Then the dinks started calling about the middle of February. Dinks asking her to go out. Dinks calling again and saying what a fun time they had. "Hey, that was a ball, wasn't it? Delightful." Laughing like girls. One dink giving her his golf scores for the week. This other dink boring the shit out of her (and Roland) with all these stock market reports. Another one, the only thing he talked about was his Donzi cigarette boat and off-shore racing, Miami-Bimini, Miami-Key West, how big the waves were, implying what a fucking hero he was out there at the helm. (Roland said to the voice on the tape, "You dink, I'd blow your ass off with a Seminole air boat. Put you smack on the trailer.") From the sound of them, it couldn't have been too hard to scare them off. The lady didn't know how lucky she was, saved from listening to them dinks.

Then the woman from the *Miami Herald* again wanting to interview her; DiCilia saying all right. Then a call from some Palm Beach magazine, the *Gold Coaster,* something like that, and Mrs. DiCilia agreeing to talk to them.

Then more conversations with Ed Grossi in May. (Roland would sit up and pay attention to these.) Then Ed inviting her to his office.

There, that was up to where Roland took over the tape concession and started getting them directly from Marta or Jesus Diaz. Nothing interesting yet, not the kind of information he was listening for.

Then the one, her call to Ed chewing him out. "I never want to see that man here again." Not loud, but a good bite in her tone. "Keep that animal away from here." (*An*imal? Hey now.) Then saying, "Why didn't you tell me yourself? Why did I have to hear it from him? Keep him away from this house. You understand?" (Roland saying, "Hey, take it easy, Karen.")

He listened to the end. Then played it back and listened again. No sir, nothing about his proposition. Not a word. Blowing off steam, but not telling the whole story, was she? Keeping a possibility open. Roland grinned.

The next few tapes, nothing of interest. One he thought at first was going to be good.

The woman talking to the operator, asking for the number of Goodman and Stern in Detroit, telling the operator it was a law office. (Uh-oh.) Then talking to a guy named Nate. Nate telling her it had been too long and how sorry he was he couldn't make Frank's funeral and was there anything he could do for her. Then Karen asking him if the name Maguire and Deep Run meant anything to him. Long pause. The guy, Nate, saying yes, he believed they handled it. Why? Karen saying it wasn't important but she'd like some information about Maguire if they had it on file. She had met him, she said, and something about Maguire wanting a job recommendation. This guy Nate saying, after another pause, well, he'd have somebody named Marshall something put a report together and send it to her. But he'd advise her to use discretion and touch base with someone at Dorado, someone close by. And how was everything else down in the land of sunshine?

"Hot in the day, cool in the evening," Roland murmured to himself. Dink lawyers, you never knew what they were talking about.

Another tape. Another conversation with Ed Grossi. Ed back from his trip. That would have been yesterday. Roland paid attention, listening carefully as Karen asked Ed about a trust fund, wanting to know what bank it was in. Ed told her.

Karen: You said in bonds, I know, but I've forgotten the name.

Ed: Miami General Revenue, at six percent.

Karen: Don't I get records, something on paper? How do I prove they're mine?

Ed: Well, as I told you, the bonds are in the name of the administrator of the estate, Dorado. The yield, the interest—what'd I say, two and a half?

("Here we go," Roland said.)

Karen: Two hundred and forty thousand.

Ed: Yeah, goes into the trust and the bank deposits it, or they credit it to your account, twenty thousand a month. Yeah, that's it.

(Roland: "That's it all right. Man, that is *it*.")

Karen: But I don't have anything that describes me as the beneficiary, or whatever I am.

Ed: You're getting the money, aren't you?

Karen: Yes, but I'd like something on paper.

Ed: I'll have Vivian get you a copy. We'll get you something, don't worry about it. How's everything else? Clara says she wants to get together with you sometime.

Karen: That'd be fine. (Long pause) Ed . . . look, we're going to have to talk about this other thing. When can I come to your office?

(Roland, writing figures on a pad of paper, looked up.)

Ed: What other thing?

Karen: Ed, for God's sake. Maybe this happens in India or Saudi Arabia, but not Fort Lauderdale, Florida. You can't simply ignore it.

Ed: Karen—

Karen: You've got to *stop* it, that's all. If you won't, I'll take you to court. I'll do *some*thing—leave here if I have to.

Ed: Karen—

Karen: If you think I'm going to live like this you're out of your mind.

Ed: All right, we'll have a talk. How about tomorrow, my office? Come on up, we'll go to lunch.

(Roland: "That's today.")

Karen: I'll meet you at Palm Bay.

(Roland: "Shit.")

He looked at his figures again, scratched them out and

started over, multiplying, dividing, trying different ways, finally, *finally* then, coming up with the answer, what twenty thousand a month was six percent of. Jesus Christ, four million dollars the woman had!

9.

Lunch at Palm Bay. Ed Grossi used a Rye Krisp and a spoon on his bowl of cottage cheese. Karen listened, sipping her Bloody Mary, picking at her shrimp salad, every once in awhile shaking her head. Unbelievable. Having to threaten, almost hit him with something to get him to talk about it.

"You serve me with some kind of cease and desist order. From doing what? Karen, this is a very personal matter. You want to get something like this in the papers?"

"If I have to. Ed, this is my life we're talking about."

Almost to himself: "People wouldn't understand it."

"Of course they wouldn't. It's something out of the Middle Ages." Karen leaned closer, staring at the quiet little man across the table. "He told you this in the hospital? Was he lucid? How do you know he was even in his right mind?"

"It was before that," Grossi said, "in my office. Before a witness."

"Who, Roland?"

"No, not Roland. I said to Frank, you're kidding. He said no, very serious. I know his voice, his tone. Nobody goes near her. I asked him why. He said I didn't have to know that. Then Vivian came in, took some dictation. She witnessed my saying yes to him, it would be done."

"Vivian, your secretary?"

"She's more my assistant."

"And Roland?"

"Somebody to carry it out, do the work."

"You trust Roland?"

"He does what he's told and keeps his mouth shut," Grossi said.

You don't know him, Karen thought, but held back from saying it. "Who else knows about it?"

"Well, Jimmy Capotorto. I told him a little, but not everything."

Karen frowned. "Who?"

"Capotorto. Frank knew him. He's been with Dorado for years; one of the associates."

"Who else?" Karen said

"That's all." Grossi paused. "But there are some stipulations I didn't mention the other day that I didn't want to get into all at once."

"Like what?" Karen said.

"Well, if you move, the payments stop. You have to live in Frank's house."

"Frank's house," Karen said. "And if I marry again —I asked you that the other day, you said you weren't sure."

"For some reason it's not a stipulation. I guess Frank assumed we'd see nobody got close to you."

"But there's nothing in the agreement that says I can't take the entire amount."

"Not in writing, no, but in the spirit of it, you might say."

"Sign the bonds over to me and let's forget the whole thing," Karen said.

Grossi said nothing, looking at Karen, then at his cottage cheese, touching it tentatively with his spoon.

"Do you know why he did it?" Karen said. "Because he was having an affair and I found out about it. With a real estate woman." A hint of amazement in her tone. "I told him—I wasn't even serious, I was mad—I told him if he was going to fool around, I would too."

"Well, he took it at face value and here we are." Grossi seemed hesitant, working something out in his mind as they sat at his regular table in the corner of the grill room. He said, "Karen, I'll tell you, something like this, I agree, it sounds like we're back in the old country."

"But we're not," Karen said; firm, knowing how far she was willing to go. "Ed, you're aware of the people in here, how they keep looking at us?"

"You get used to it."

"I go to the john I get looks, I hear my name, Mrs. Frank DiCilia, yes, that's her, people talking about me, not going to much trouble to hide it."

"Sure, you're like a movie star."

"All right, what if I stood up right now and made a speech," Karen said. "Tapped my glass with a spoon—'May I have your attention, please? I want to tell you something you're not going to believe, but it's the honest-to-God truth, every word.' "

"Karen, come on."

"Come on where? Goddamn it, I'm not going to play your game. I'm not in the fucking Mafia or whatever you don't call it. What do you expect me to do?"

"Keep it down a little, all right? I understand how you feel."

"Like hell you do."

"Yes, I do." Grossi nodding patiently. "Listen to me a minute. I acknowledge his wish, I'm thinking, Jesus Christ, nobody ever wanted something like this before. I try to remember. Maybe a long time ago, I don't know."

"But it doesn't matter, because you do whatever he says." Karen holding on, refusing to let go. "He tells you to kill somebody—what's the difference?"

"Karen"—the tired voice—"what is that? You think it's a big thing? Maybe sometimes it is, but there's a reason for everything. The man has a reason, I don't have to ask him why."

She leaned close to the table. "I told you why. Because he has this thing in his head about paying back."

"Listen to me and let me finish," Grossi said. "Even when I don't want anything to do with it, I have to satisfy my conscience I've done something, I've acknowledged, I've gone through the motions. You understand? Then I say to myself, okay, that's all you can do. You can't watch her the rest of your life. I say to myself, did he mean that long? Forever? I answer no, of course not. I get a heart attack, cancer, I'm gone. Who continues the agreement? Jimmy Capotorto? Well, if I tell him to, but what does he care? He's got enough to think about. So how can it be forever? I say, Frank wanted to teach her a lesson. All right, there's the lesson. Did she learn it? I don't know. Like a teacher—did the student learn it? What can the teacher do? So, I say, it's up to her, she knows what's going on. She knows his wish, stay away from men even after his death. Does she want to honor his wish? I say to myself, not to you, not to anybody else, only to myself. Maybe it should be up to her now. Something between her and her husband."

There was a silence.

"You have more to do than keep watch on me," Karen said.

Grossi nodded.

"Assign the bonds over and let's stop all this."

"I have to think about it a little more."

"But you will keep Roland away from me."

"Don't worry about Roland."

She sat quietly, aware of sounds, voices around her. She waited, wanting to be sure. Ed Grossi touched the cottage cheese again with his spoon, then put the spoon down and picked up his napkin.

"I won't have to go to court then," Karen said.

"No, you won't have to go to court, if you give me time, let me be sure in my mind it's all right."

"Thank you," Karen said.

Maguire's body, arms raised, a piece of fish in each hand, formed a Y. He stood on the footrung of an aluminum pole that dug into his groin, the pole extending from a platform on a slight angle, so that Maguire's fish-offerings were held some fifteen feet above the surface of the Flying Dolphin Show tank.

He said to the mothers and fathers and children lining the cement rail, "Okay . . . now this double hand-feeding can be a little tricky, considering the height"—looking up—"*and* the wind conditions today. The dolphins could collide in midair, with a combined weight of"—serious, almost grim—"nine hundred pounds. And you know who's gonna be under them if they do. Yours truly, standing up here trying to look cool. Okay . . . here they come. Bonnie on my right, Pebbles on my left—"

Or was it the other way around?

The pair of dolphin rose glistening wet-gray in the sunlight, took the fish from his hands and peeled off, arching back into the water.

"And they got it! How about that, fifteen feet in the air. Wasn't that great? Let's hear it for Bonnie *and* . . . Peb-bles."

Applause, as Maguire stepped down off the pole to the platform. He got three hunks of cod from his fish-bucket, quickly threw two of them out to Bonnie and Pebbles, and waited for Mopey Dick.

Come on—

Mopey's head rose from the water, below the platform. A wet raspberries sound came from Mopey's blowhole.

"What? You didn't like the double jump, Mopey?"

Rattles and clicks and whines from the blowhole. The kids watching, looking over the rail, loved it.

"You say you can jump higher?"

More rattles and clicks.

"Well, let's just see about that." Maguire sidearmed Mopey the piece of fish he was holding, stooped to the bucket and selected a long tailpiece. "You think you're so good, let's see you come up *six*teen feet and take the fish out of my mouth. Okay, Mopey? Everybody want to see him try it?"

Of course. The kids yelling, "Yeaaaaaaa—" as Maguire, with a piece of dead fish hanging from his mouth, adjusted the pole, raising it a foot, thinking, Jesus Christ—

Karen came out of the round white building, Neptune's Realm, down from the Flying Dolphin Show. She waited on the walk, looking around, as the moms and dads with their cameras and kids moved on to the Shark Lagoon.

There he was. Across the lawn, walking with a girl brushing her hair. Both wearing the white shorts and red T-shirts. He must have come out another exit. Karen watched them go through the fence enclosing the shark pool. Maguire mounted the structure that was like a diving platform, playing out a mike cord behind him. The girl remained below: cute little thing with a lot of Farrah Fawcett hair. Karen wondered how old the girl was. Not much more than twenty. She noticed Maguire was quite tan, healthy looking; different than the man she remembered sitting in the dark. She approached the crowd that rimmed part of the cement lagoon. There was an island in the middle, a palm tree and several sleepy pelicans. Sharks moved through the murky water like brown shadows.

He looked younger in his white shorts. Good legs. His voice was different, coming out of the P.A. system. It sounded like a recording.

"Nurse sharks do not have a reputation as maneaters, but like all sharks they're very unpredictable. They might not eat for three months, then go into a feeding frenzy at any time. What Lesley is doing is jiggling that ladyfish on the end of the line to simulate a dying fish, which gives out low-frequency sound waves that can be detected by a shark as far as . . . nine . . . hundred . . . yards away. There's a shark coming in from the left . . . Look at that."

Karen watched Maguire, then let her gaze move over the crowd, pausing on some of the men. Which one would you pick as an armed robber? Maguire would be about the last one.

"Well, this time for bait we're going to use . . . Lesley. Yes, Lesley is going down *in*to the lagoon in an attempt to hand-feed a shark with her bare hand . . .

using no glove or shark repellant of any kind or . . . feed a barehand *to* a shark if she isn't careful."

The girl's face raised, giving Maguire a deadpan look. Karen saw it. For some reason she thought of Ed Grossi, Ed eating his cottage cheese with a spoon—an hour ago at Palm Bay.

Then coming over the S.E. 17th Street Causeway and seeing the sign, SEASCAPE. Why not? She felt like doing something. She felt thoroughly herself, almost relaxed, for the first time in a week. And probably the only woman here in a dress. Beige linen, gold chain and bracelet. She should have gone home first and changed—remembering him saying, "Practically around the corner," and telling him she had never been here.

He was saying to his audience, "We're not having a whole lot of luck getting the sharks into the feeding area. As I mentioned they can go as long as three months without feeding. There's one . . . no, changed his mind. Well . . . let's give Lesley a big hand for getting down in the shark lagoon"—pause—"she may need one some day."

"You sounded a lot different," Karen said.

"I know," Maguire said. "I hear my voice on the P.A., I think it's somebody else. You want a Coke or something?"

"Don't you have to work?"

"The main event's on next. Go over there—see the yellow and white awning? I'll meet you there in a couple of minutes. He seemed glad to see her, but hesitant, almost shy.

Karen got two Cokes and sat down at a picnic table away from the cement walk and the refreshment counter behind the grandstand. She heard, over the P.A. system, "Good afternoon ladies and gentlemen, boys and girls. Welcome to Brad Allen's World-Famous Seascape Porpoise and Sea-Lion Show." Pause. "And now, heeeeeeeeere's Brad!"

Karen said, "Was that you?" as Maguire sat down across from her.

"I'm afraid so."

"You always do it the same way?"

"Well—no, not always."

"The other night, I couldn't imagine you working here."

"No—"

"I wasn't inferring anything by that."

"No, I understand. I'm a little out of place, but nobody's caught on yet."

"Maybe I know you better than most people," Karen said. "Do you like doing this?"

"It's all right. It beats tending bar."

"Why don't you quit?"

"I'm thinking about it."

"Did you—" Karen paused. "Well, it's none of my business. I wondered if you sent your friends their share."

"Yeah, their wives. I sent 'em money orders. They can use it."

On the P.A. system in the background, Brad Allen was introducing Pepper, Dixie, and Bonzai to the audience.

"I still don't know the difference between a porpoise and a dolphin," Karen said. "You never told me, did you?"

"No, I guess we got into other things." Looking away from her and then back, hesitantly.

He'd been doing that since she approached him. Natural, but just a little shy. She liked it and smiled when he said, "You didn't have to get all dressed up to come here."

"I was having lunch with a friend. Then coming over the causeway I saw the sign and thought, Does he really work there or not?"

"See? I wouldn't lie to you."

"I love your routine. Do you ever vary it?"

"Only when I forget lines. Or leave something out."

Brad Allen was telling his audience that Lolly the sea lion was now going to balance the ball and *walk* on her front flippers. "Heeeeey, look at that!"

"I don't think you're going to last here," Karen said. "I mean I wouldn't think you'd be able to take it as a steady diet."

"No—" He smiled, shaking his head. "You're right."

"What will you do then?"

"I don't know. Go down to Key West, see if it's changed any."

"Not back to Detroit?"

"I doubt it."

"We haven't discussed Detroit yet," Karen said. "Have we?"

"What's to discuss? Have you ever been to Belle Isle? Greenfield Village?"

"How about where you went to school." No—she shouldn't have said that. Then, what year, getting into ages. He was younger than she was. A few years, anyway.

"I went to De LaSalle," Maguire said. "By the City Airport."

She had meant college; he was referring to a high school. "I know where it is," Karen said. "I lived on the east side."

"Where'd you go?"

"Dominican."

"You're a Catholic?" He seemed surprised.

"Sort of. Not the kind I used to be."

"Yeah, I've fallen off myself. It's funny, isn't it?"

"What is?"

"I mean I'd never of thought of you as a Catholic. Even with your name."

"Or with yours," Karen said. "The thing that messes up yours is the Calvin."

He was looking directly at her now.

"How old are you?"

Without a pause Karen said, "Thirty-eight. How old are you?"

"Thirty-six."

"You don't look it."

"You don't either," Maguire said.

She should have told him thirty-six.

He said, "I told them I was thirty when I came to work here; everybody looked so young. I almost—just now I almost said I was thirty-two. Why would I do that?"

"Well, no one wants to get old."

"But thirty-six, thirty-eight, that's not old. I figure it's about the best age there is."

"It's all right," Karen said, thinking, Thirty-eight; what year was I born? "I don't give it much thought one way or the other. You're as old as you feel."

"Right," Maguire said. "Usually I feel about eighteen."

"I like twenty-five," Karen said. "I wouldn't mind being twenty-five again. Do it right this time."

"What would you do different?"

"Lots of things. I'd travel first, before I settled down anywhere."

"Why don't you do it now?"

"I may."

"I've traveled," Maguire said, "but mostly between here and Colorado. I've been to Mexico. Next—in fact, I was gonna get a passport." He paused. "Then something came up."

"Where were you going?"

"Spain. The South of France, around in there. Get a car and drive, like Madrid to Rome. That sounds pretty good."

"I've always wanted to go to Madrid," Karen said. "Málaga—"

"You've never been over there?"

"We used to go to the Greenbriar. Or SAE conventions."

"Frank DiCilia did?"

"The other Frank, the first one. The second one, I couldn't get him out of Florida."

"Except go to Detroit now and then," Maguire said, "if I recall you saying."

"Eastern nine-five-two, Miami to Detroit, the dinner flight. Nine-five-three back again."

"Well, what do you sit around in that big house for, if you've got the urge and you can go anywhere you want?"

"Right," Karen said. "It's dumb, isn't it?"

"You want to have dinner with me tonight?" Maguire said. "Anywhere you want. I just came into some money."

Three times Roland dropped the wrought-iron knocker against the front door. When Marta appeared, he pushed the door all the way open and walked in past her.

"Missus isn't here."

Roland walked through the sitting room to the French doors and looked out on the patio.

"Where she at?"

"Missus isn't here."

Roland came back to the front hall and crossed to look into the living room, narrowing his eyes at the size of it—the white plaster walls and beamed cathedral ceiling—as if to make the room smaller and spot her hiding someplace.

"Where is she?"

As he moved toward the stairway, Marta said, "Let me see, please, if she is upstairs."

Roland said, "You stay here, honey. You call anybody on the phone I'll know about it, won't I?" He reached down as Gretchen came running across the polished floor to him. "Hey, Gretchie, how you doin' huh? How you doin', girl? You gettin' much?"

Karen was thinking, Thirty-eight from seventy-nine . . . forty-one.

Lying on the king-size bed in her robe, on top of the spread, ankles crossed, resting before her bath.

She would have been a war baby instead of a Depression baby. Forty-one and seventeen . . . fifty-eight. Graduated from high school in '58. From Michigan in '62. It wasn't going to work. Unless she was married to Frank—thinking of the first Frank—say, eleven years. That would make Julie—married, living in L.A. —about fifteen.

So don't mention Julie. Except what if he says—

She had already told him.

The other night, listing the two Franks, yes, and a daughter—my daughter the actress. Shit. She had already mentioned Julie.

All right. She could have been married at Ann Arbor, still in school. Say, freshman year. If Julie was born in '60, she'd be nineteen now.

Better stay away from it. Change the subject if he brings up Julie.

Somebody was coming upstairs. Marta?

Avoid talking about age or tell him the truth. What difference did it make? She wasn't even sure why she was going out with him. She liked him; he was different; relaxed, low-key but very aware. She liked him—it was strange—quite a lot. Right from the beginning. But how did you make room for someone like Maguire? How did you explain him? Walking into the Palm Bay Club—

"Hey, look-it her waiting for me!"

Roland was in the room. She saw his hat, the color of his suit. She saw him coming, arms raised, *diving* at her! Karen screamed. She rolled, reaching for the edge of the bed, and Roland landed next to her with the sound of the frame cracking, ripping away from the oak headboard, collapsing, the king-size boxspring and mattress dropping abruptly within the frame, to the floor.

Roland, on his elbows, close to her, hat low over his eyes, grinned at her.

"How you doin'?"

Karen screamed. "Marta!"

She tried to roll off the edge, but he caught her and

held her to the bed beneath one arm across her stomach.

"Take off my hat for me."

"Get *out* of here!" And screamed again, "Marta!"

"I told her we wouldn't need anything."

Roland took his hat by the brim and sailed it away from the bed. His arm came down again to grab her as she tried to twist away, free herself, and now he lowered his face to her, nuzzling it against her neck, working aside the collar of the robe. "I ain't gonna hurt you. This hurt?" His voice softly muffled. "Feels kinda good, don't it." His face moving lower as he pulled her toward him to lie on her back, his face nuzzling into the robe.

Karen held herself rigid, staring at the ceiling, feeling his mouth on her, his face moving side to side, opening her robe. She could hear Gretchen in the room, license and ID tags jingling on her collar.

"We don't have nothing on under there, do we? Mmmmmm, you sure smell nice." He looked up then, turning his cheek to her. "Here, smell mine. Called Manpower. Little girl in the store said, 'For the man who knows what he wants.' You like it?"

Karen turned her face away, the perfumed astringent scent almost making her gag. Thinking, Don't move. Don't fight. Breathe. His face moved lower, and she was staring at the ceiling again, feeling his mouth, feeling her heart beating beneath his mouth.

"Don't that feel goooood? Yeaaaah, feels good have somebody holding you again, don't it? Been a long, long time." His mouth moving over her, voice drowsy, soft.

Thinking, Six months. Seven months. Thinking, There's nothing you can do. Close your eyes. It could be—his mouth moving—it could be anyone. It could be someone else. But her eyes remained open.

*Any*one else, for God's sake. But it wasn't going to be this one!

Karen rolled into him, jabbed against him as hard as she could and abruptly rolled the other way, reached the edge of the bed with her knee and one hand before he caught her again and she could feel the bulk of him, his weight, against her back.

"Where you goin', sugar?"

"I'm getting up."

"What for? You got to make we-we?"

"I'm going to call Ed Grossi."

"Hey, shit, you don't want to bother Ed. This here's between you and me. You feel it?" He pushed against her. "That's what's between us, if you wondered I had something in my pocket. You want me to tell you what it is?"

Karen didn't answer.

"It's my Louisville Slugger."

"You know I'm going to tell Ed," Karen said, seeing Gretchen now, white whiskers and sad eyes looking up at her, only a few feet away. "You must be out of your mind."

"With love," Roland said. "Listen, come on. I wouldn't hurt you for the world."

"I saw Ed today."

"You had a nice lunch, did you?"

Karen hesitated. How would he know tnat? She almost asked him; but it had nothing to do with right now, with Roland pressing against her.

She said, "I think you'd better talk to Ed as soon as you can. You're going to be in a lot of trouble."

"I don't mind trouble. Shit, I like a little trouble. Keeps you thinking."

She wanted to jab her elbow into him as hard as she could, but she held on, keeping an even tone as she said, "Talk to him. He's agreed, I'm not going to be watched any more. The whole arrangement—it's over with."

Roland lay heavily against her, silent for a moment. "No shit, Ed's calling it off?"

"Talk to him, will you please?"

"You cry on his shoulder or kick him in the nuts? Either way, I believe, might work."

"Call him. The phone's right behind you."

There was a silence again.

"But did he check with Frank? What's Frank say about it?"

"Let me up, all right?"

Roland took his time. As he rolled away from her, Karen was off the bed, pulling her robe together, moving across the room.

"Hold it there, sweet potato. Don't go running off. I want to tell you something."

"And I want you to leave. Right now."

Roland got up slowly. "Messed up your bed, didn't I?"

"Don't worry about the bed. Just leave."

"I can probably fix it for you."

"Please, I'm asking you—"

Roland picked up his hat. He walked over to the wall of mirrors that enclosed Karen's closet. "See, what Ed says, like half the time don't mean diddly-shit. Ed's getting old, little guinea brain becoming shriveled up from all that red wine."

"Please. Talk to him yourself, all right?"

"See, but it ain't up to Ed. What Frank DiCilia wants, it's still like hanging out there in the air somewheres. Frank didn't say okay, never mind. Just Ed said it. But Ed, his thinking's all fucked up, ain't it? So that means I have to take over." Looking at himself in the floor-to-ceiling mirror, setting his Ox Bow straw just right, little lower in front. "And see nobody gets close to you." Looking at Karen in the mirror now, Karen by the foot of the bed. "You follow me? Nothing's changed. You start seeing somebody, the fella's likely to get one of his bones broke, and he won't even know what for."

Karen said, "You know I'm going to call Ed."

Roland shrugged. "And he'll shake his little guinea finger at me. But you know I'll still be comin' around, won't I? And long as I do, I'm your big chance."

Roland winked at her in the mirror.

10.

Maguire looked up the number, then had to go over to the TV set to turn down the volume. "Okay? Just for a minute." Aunt Leona sat watching Barbara Walters talking to Anwar Sadat; she didn't say anything.

It was ten to seven.

"Hi. It looks like I'm gonna be a little late. This girl lives next door said I could use her car; but she went somewhere. She isn't back yet."

"That's all right," Karen said. "Listen, why don't we make it some other time then?"

"The car's not that important," Maguire said. "I wanted to pick you up, but if I can't—we can meet somewhere, can't we?'

There was a pause.

"I guess we could."

"What's the matter?"

"Nothing. I was trying to think of a place."

"You sound different," Maguire said.

"Where do you want to meet?"

What was it? She sounded tired.

"If I don't call you back by . . . seven-thirty, how about if we meet at the Yankee Clipper? Is that all right?"

"Fine."

"You don't sound very enthusiastic about it."

"Really, that's fine. I'll see you there."

"About eight, if I don't call—"

She had hung up.

Jesus Diaz wore a clean yellow sportshirt and his white poplin jacket to go to 1 Isla Bahía. At twenty after seven he rang the bell at the side door. Marta let her brother in without a word, left him to wait in the kitchen several minutes, returned and handed him the day's cassette tape.

"What's the matter?" Jesus said.

"Your friend Roland, what else."

"He's not my friend."

"The pimp, he came today and attempted to rape her."

"How do you know?"

"I heard it, how do I know. He broke the bed. Two hundred years old, he broke it jumping on her."

"Maybe she wanted him to," Jesus said.

"Go," Marta said. "Get out of here."

Roland was on the balcony of his eight hundred-dollar-a-month Miami Shores apartment that had a view down the street to the ocean, drinking beer with his boots off, feet in blue silk socks propped on the railing. He let Jesus Diaz in, took Ralph Stanley and the Clinch Mountain Boys off the hi-fi and plugged in his tape player-recorder.

"Lemme have it."

They listened to a woman's voice say, "Dorado Management . . . No, I'm sorry, Mr. Grossi has left for the day."

Jesus saw Roland wink at him; he didn't know why.

Another woman's voice said, "Hello?" . . . "Clara, is Ed there? It's Karen."

No, Ed had gone to some kind of business meeting. Roland thought they might talk awhile, but Karen asked her to have Ed call and that was it.

Then the next voice, a man's, said, "Hi. It looks like I'm gonna be a little late."

Roland listened and played it again. He said, "Son of a *bitch.*" Looked at his watch and then at Jesus Diaz. "Yankee Clipper. Go see who he is."

"It's only the first time. Maybe it's nothing," Jesus said.

"How you know it's the first time?"

"I don't know his name. Like the other ones on the phone."

"Follow him then. See where he lives, look it up in the city directory."

"Maybe he rents a place."

"Jesus Christ," Roland said, "then find out where he works. You understand what I mean? Follow the dink till you find out about him. Let me know tomorrow, and I'll tell you what to do."

Jesus Diaz wanted to ask something about Mrs. DiCilia, but he didn't know how to say it. So he left to go to the Yankee Clipper.

They sat next to each other at a banquette table facing the bar and the portholes back of it that presented an illuminated, underwater view of the hotel swimming pool.

Karen said, "I just realized why you come here."

"I've never been here before."

"The windows, like in the dolphin tank."

"You're changing the subject again."

"No—I just noticed it."

"I'm not dumb—" Maguire stopped, reconsidering. "I mean I'm not that dumb. This afternoon you're very relaxed, you talk, you're interested. I call you—since then you're like a different person. More like at your house the other night. No, different. You're quieter. But tense like you were then, something on your mind."

"Okay, I have something on my mind," Karen said. Sitting next to him, she could look at the bar, the portholes, the people in the room, without obviously avoiding his eyes. Or she could look down at her menu open against the table, resting on her lap. "That happens, doesn't it? A minor problem comes up, something you have to work out."

"I don't think it's minor," Maguire said.

"There's a man at the bar, the one in the white jacket. I think I know him," Karen said, "but I can't remember where."

Maguire raised his hand to the waitress, impatient,

trying to appear calm, glancing at the guy sitting sideways to the bar—*him?*—then looking up as the waitress came over. "Two more please, same way."

"That was two Beefeater on the rocks?"

The waitress checked their glasses, leaving Karen's. "Beefeater and a white rum martini."

The waitress turned away and he said to Karen, "Look, I don't care about the guy at the bar—"

"I know who he is," Karen said. "Marta's brother."

"Okay," Maguire said. "I don't care about Marta's brother. I don't want to look at the menu yet, I just want to know what's the matter. Even if it's none of my business. The other night you hint around like you want to tell me something. You show me a *gun,* you want to know how to use it. I'll admit something to you. I purposely didn't ask you the other night, because how do I know what I'm walking into? I'll tell you something else. I've been arrested nine times and not one conviction. I mean not even a suspended. All kinds of sheets on me, but no convictions. The last time, I promised—I even prayed, which I hadn't done in, what, twenty years. Get me out of this one and I'll never . . . get in trouble again. I'll dedicate myself to clean living and not even *talk* to anybody who's been in that other life. So the other night—you don't mind my saying, with your husband's associations and all, here's Frank DiCilia's wife wants to know how to use a gun. She must have all the protection she needs, her husband's friends still around—what does she want a gun for? See, that's where I was the other night. But now I'm asking you what the problem is. I don't know why, maybe this afternoon did something. You came to see me, you were very warm and open. That's another thing. I feel something with you. I feel close, and I want to help you if I can."

"You were different this afternoon," Karen said. "You seemed almost shy."

"I don't know, maybe I was a little self-conscious in my camp outfit, you seeing me there. But now I've got my outfit on I feel good in. See, I'm *me* in this outfit.

Tan and blue, it doesn't matter that it's cheap or what anybody thinks of it, I feel good in it, I feel like the original *me* before I ever screwed up or wasted time. Does that make sense? I don't know—"

"I should've worn mine." Karen was looking at him now, smiling. "You were funny this afternoon, with your carnival voice."

"And now I'm frustrated," Maguire said. "I want to know what's going on."

The martini made her feel warm, protected. Still looking at him she said, "You have blue eyes," a little surprised.

"See?" Maguire said. "We're both from the east side of Detroit, we're both sort of Catholic and have blue eyes. What else do you need?"

"There's a man," Karen said, and paused. "I think he's going to ask me for money. Quite a lot of money. And if I don't give it to him, I think he's going to kill me." Still looking at him. "You tell me what else I need."

"Me," Maguire said.

Jesus Diaz ordered another Tom Collins, his fifth one, the bartender giving him the nothing-look again, not saying "Here you are," or "Thank you, sir," or anything, not saying a word. The bartender looked like a guy named Tommy Laglesia he had fought at the Convention Center ten years ago and lost in the fifth on a TKO. If the bartender did thank him or say something like that, the bartender had better be careful of his tone. Jesus would take the man by the hair, pull his face down hard against the bar and say, "You welcome."

Shit. He was tired of looking at the empty green water in the windows, waiting for a swimmer to appear, a girl. Tired of looking around, pretending to look at nothing. He didn't like to drink this much. But what was he supposed to do, sitting at a bar? What else would he be here for? While they sat over there drinking. Nine-thirty, they hadn't eaten dinner yet, Jesus

Diaz thinking, I'm going to be drunk. We are all going to be drunk. The two drinking and talking close together, looking at each other, talking very seriously, the woman talking most of the time, the man in tan and blue smoking cigarettes, talking a little, touching the woman's hand, leaving his hand on hers. Like lovers. Man, he was fast if they were lovers. Jesus Diaz had never seen him before. Maybe he was an old lover from before, a lover from when she was married to DiCilia, yes, someone younger than the old man. Young lover but old friend. That's what he must be.

Ten-fifteen, still not eating. Not touching their drinks either. Now only a small amount remaining in the sixth Tom Collins, the fucking bartender who looked like Tommy Laglesia pretending not to be looking at him. Come over and say something, Jesus was thinking; tired, ready to go to sleep on the bar.

Almost ten-thirty. They were leaving. They must have already paid the girl without him seeing it. They were getting up, leaving!

The fucking bartender was down at the other end. Of course, talking to someone who wouldn't stop talking. Jesus Diaz stood up on the rung of the barstool.

"Hey!"

The bartender came to him and this time he said, "Like another?"

"Shit no," Jesus Diaz said. "I want to get out of this fucking place."

"We've got to eat something," Karen said. "Three martinis—you know what that does to me?"

"Four," Maguire said. "It makes you feel good."

They stood on the patio making up their minds, sit down or go back in. There was a breeze off the channel, the feeling of the ocean close by.

"No worries," Karen said. "No, you still have them, but they don't seem as real. Maybe that's the answer. Stay in the bag and forget about it. Whenever he comes over, Marta can tell him Missus has passed out. So—do you feel like a drink?"

"Not right now."

"Something to eat then? Why didn't we eat?"

"Lost interest, I guess. I'm still not hungry."

Maguire was looking toward the house, at the dark archway and the French doors. A lamp was on in the sitting room. He could see the back of the Louis XVI bergère. The windows of the living room were dark; the upstairs windows dark, except for one. He could feel her next to him. She was wearing a dark buttoned-up sweater now, over the dress he thought of as a long shirt, open at the neck, letting him see the beginning soft-curve of her breast when they were sitting at the table. He took her arm, and they began to walk out on the lawn toward the seawall.

"That's one way," he said. "Get stoned. But the other way, going to the cops—I'm not prejudiced, I just don't see it'll do any good. Unless he's awful dumb."

"He acts dumb," Karen said, "but I'm not sure. He's so confident."

"I doubt the cops'd put him under surveillance. They'll tell you they'll serve him with a peace bond and that should do it. Like a warning, stay away from her. But it doesn't mean anything because how're they gonna enforce it? He comes here. You call the cops. They come and he's gone. They pick him up, he says, 'Who, me? I never threatened the lady.' They shake their finger at him, 'Stay away from her.' That's about all they can do. But the way it is, he hasn't asked for anything yet."

"No."

"So it's not extortion. How do you know he wants money?"

"What else is there?"

"I don't know," Maguire said, "but I think he's interested in you more than the money. Or you *and* the money."

"You're kidding."

"Why not? What does he do? He worked for your husband?"

"He works for Ed Grossi, but I doubt if he will much longer."

"Why not?"

"*Why?* After what he did?"

"He jumped on your bed," Maguire said. "You can say he had rape in his eyes, but in the light of what he does for Ed Grossi—we don't know but it might be very heavy work, a key job—then all he did was jump on your bed. Ed Grossi says, 'Don't worry, I'll talk to him.' And he says to Roland, 'Quit jumping on the lady's bed, asshole,' and that's it."

"Ed's a friend of mine," Karen said.

"That's nice," Maguire said, "but in his business you're a friend when he's got time or if it isn't too much trouble; unless you're in the business with him and you've taken the oath or whatever they do—even then, I don't know."

Karen thought about it, walking slowly in the darkness, holding her arms now, inside herself.

"What if I told Ed, I insist I be there when he speaks to Roland?"

"Fine," Maguire said. "Then they put on this show. Take *that,* and *that.* Ed chews him out and Roland stands there cracking his knuckles. Even if Ed's serious, he wants the guy to stay away from you, how important is the guy to Ed? Or how much control does he have over him? That's the question."

They stopped near the seawall, looking out at the lights of the homes across the channel.

"Are you cold?"

"Hold me," Karen said. "Will you?"

He put his arms around her, and she pressed in against him. She felt small. He thought she would fit the way Lesley did and feel much the same as Lesley, but she was smaller, more delicate; she felt good against him. He wanted to hold her very close without hurting her. He became aware of something else—though maybe it was only in his mind—that this was a woman and Lesley was a girl. Was there a difference? He raised her face with his hand and kissed her. She put her head against his cheek, then raised her face, their eyes holding for a moment, almost smiling, and they began to kiss again, their mouths fitting together and then moving, taking parts of each other's mouths, no Lesley comparison now, Lesley gone, the woman taking over alone, the woman eager, he could feel it, but holding back a little, patient. There was a difference.

He said, "Why don't you show me the bed."

She said, "All right—"

"Do you know what I thought about? The maid catching us. Why? It's my house, I can do anything I want."

"Afraid she'll go down to Southwest Eighth Street, tell everybody."

They lay close, legs touching, the sheet pulled up now.

"But only for a minute," Karen said.

"What?"

"That I worried about the maid. By the time we got to the stairs I couldn't wait."

"I couldn't wait to see you," Maguire said. His hand moved over her thigh to her patch of hair and rested there gently. "To look at your face and look at you here"—his hand moving, stroking her— "and see both of you. I tried to imagine, before, what it would look like."

"Really? You do that?"

"No, not all the time. Most girls, I look at them and I'm not interested in what it looks like. I *know,* for some reason and, well, it's just there. It's okay but it's not that important. But every once in awhile I look at a particular girl, a woman, and I don't know what hers looks like, because it's a very special one, it's *hers,* it's part of her and—I can't explain it. But that particular person I know I can feel very close to."

"And I'm one of those?"

"There aren't that many. Just once in awhile I see a girl, a woman—"

"You're having trouble putting me in an age group,"

Karen said. "It's okay, girl, woman. Which do you want me to be?"

"No, see, I like the word *girl*. Giiirl, it's a good word. Woman, I think of a cleaning woman."

"And you like girls."

"Yeah, but I'm not preoccupied, if that's what you mean."

"What about the shark girl? Let's give her a hand because she may need one someday?"

"Oh. Lesley." That was one thing about girls, women, he'd never understand. How they could read your mind. "Lesley's"—what was she?—"sort of spoiled. She pouts, puts on this act if she doesn't get her way. Or, she's arrogant, very dramatic, and you have to wait around for her to come back to earth."

"Do you go out with her?"

"Well, I have. She's the one who lives next door. In fact it's her aunt's place, the Casa Loma. She got me the apartment. It's an efficiency really."

"Oh," Karen said.

"That's all. I ride to work with her."

"She's a cute girl."

"I guess so. If you like that type."

"Do you picture her pubic hair?"

Jesus Christ—

"No. She's not the type I picture. She's more what they're turning out today. Not a lot of individuality, but a lot of hair and a cute ass. If that turns you on, fine."

"Does she turn you on?"

"Lesley? I ride to work with her, ride home. We talk once in awhile."

"But does she turn you on?"

"The only reason you pick her, you happened to've seen me with her."

"Are there many others?"

"No, what I mean, it's like if I picked out Roland because we were talking about him and I ask you, when he jumped in bed with you, did it turn you on?"

"He jumped *on* the bed."

"Yeah, but did it?"

"We sound like we're married," Karen said.

"This is what it's like, huh? I always wondered if I was missing something."

She turned her head on the pillow to look at him. "I think you were miscast. You should've been something else."

"Yeah, like what?"

"I haven't decided yet. But—you would've ended up in prison. You're smart enough to know that."

"That's why I got out of it."

"No, I think you're out of it because you finally realized you never should've been in. That's what I mean you were miscast. Some wild idea influenced you."

"Money," Maguire said.

"See, you pretend you're cynical, but you're not. It wasn't just money. Maybe the risk, or the excitement."

"Maybe," Maguire said. "I remember telling Andre I could do without anymore thrills. Yeah, maybe you're right," his tone thoughtful, going back in his mind and beginning to wonder how he'd got into the life—always one more, just to raise traveling money—and how those years had gone by so fast. He said, "That wasn't me I was telling you about. It must've been somebody else."

Looking at him lying next to her in her bed she could say to herself, My God, who is this guy? Or she could say, Somebody I've known for a long time. She said to him, "You feel it, don't you? You said you felt close." Putting her hand on his hand.

"Like the other night was years ago," Maguire said. "Even dinner, the one we didn't have, seems a long time ago now."

"That's what I'll tell Marta, we're old friends," Karen said, and smiled. "Why do I worry about Marta? Even with Frank, I was never afraid to stand up to him."

"I guess you did," Maguire said.

"But I was always worried—not worried, concerned, with what the maid thought of me."

"Because you think of her as a person and not just a maid," Maguire said. "Talk about miscast, the lady of the house. I don't see you that way at all. A *lady,* yeah, I suppose, the way it's used. But I don't see you just sitting around pouring tea."

"How do you see me?"

"Well, like in a sweater and jeans, doing something outside." He paused. "You want me to tell you, really?"

"Yes, I'd love to know."

"I see *us,*" Maguire said. "I see us driving through Spain. I see us at a sidewalk table, place with a red awning. I see us looking at somebody, like some tourist, and nudging each other and laughing."

She turned to him as he spoke, moving closer and laying her hand on his chest.

"I see us picking up our maps and a couple bottles of red wine to take with us."

"What kind of car do we have?"

"Alpha Romeo. Convertible, with the top down."

"Where're we going?"

"Madrid to the Costa del Sol. And if we don't like it, we'll go to some other costa."

"I think we'll like it," Karen said.

She thought, briefly, But who's paying for it?

Then put it out of her mind. She felt safe. For the time being, she could close her eyes without imagining something happening to her. She could picture herself doing whatever she wanted. She tried to imagine the sidewalk cafe and the Alpha Romeo. But she saw herself coming out of a shop on Worth Avenue, Palm Beach, putting on her sunglasses, and someone saying, That's Karen DiCilia.

11.

"Then they go back to her house," Jesus Diaz said to Roland. "Then, you know, after awhile, he goes home."

Roland was down on the floor in his undershorts doing pushups, red-faced, tight-jawed, counting, "Ninety-five . . . ninety-six . . . Where's he live?" straining to say it.

Like the time on the toilet, Jesus Diaz thought. The time Roland, sitting on the toilet, grunting, making noises, had made him stand in the doorway of the bathroom while Roland talked to him.

"He lives up by Northeast Twenty-ninth Street, in Fort Lauderdale."

"One hunnert," Roland said, getting up, breathing heavily with his hands on his hips. Jesus Diaz tried to read what was printed in red on the front of Roland's white bikini undershorts, without staring at his crotch.

"You tell me she met him at the place. So then they both drive to her house?"

"No, he went in the car with her, the Mercedes."

"Then how'd he get home?"

What was printed on Roland's shorts, was *Home of the Whopper*. Jesus Diaz said, "He drove her car home."

"She let him use her car?"

"I guess so. He drove it to where he work, that place, Seascape."

Roland squinted. "Seascape? The fuck is Seascape?"

"That kind of porpoise place. They have the shows there."

"Jesus Christ," Roland said. "Seascape, yeah. I believe Dorado owns it, or did. What's he do there?"

"The tricks, you know, with the porpoise. Make them jump up, take a piece of fish out of his mouth. All like that."

"Well, you go on back and see him," Roland said. "Take somebody with you to hold his arms."

"Today you mean?"

"I mean right now, partner. Get on it."

"Man, I'd like to get some sleep first."

"What you need sleep for? Didn't you go to bed?"

"I'm just tired," Jesus Diaz said, and left to go do his job, tired or not.

Do it right or Roland would chew his ass out, tell him to quit chasing that Cuban *cocha.* Stay in shape like him.

Sure, but if he'd said he was awake all night, except for dozing off—sitting in the mangrove bushes across the street so the security car wouldn't see him—then Roland would say, All *night?* You mean to say the dink spent the *night?* Then Roland might go over there and do something to the woman again.

Man, he was tired though.

Go home, get the Browning to put under his jacket, just in case. Pick up Lionel Oliva at the Tall Pines Trailer Park; pull him out of bed. Hey, Lionel, you want to beat up somebody for a hundred dollars? How big? Not big. Shit yes, he'd jump in the car. It shouldn't be hard. The porpoise man didn't look very strong. Also he'd be tired out after his night in the two-hundred-year-old bed.

Marta had said, handing the early-morning cup of coffee to him out the side door, "If it wasn't broken before, it is now." Saying it, not as a truth, but because she was happy for the woman.

Jesus Diaz was happy for her also. It was too bad he had to do this to her old friend.

Maguire said to the crowd on the top deck of the Flying Dolphin tank, "There's the trick it took us eighteen months to teach him. He lays on his side, raises one flipper and . . . that's it. You can see why we call him *Mopey* . . . Dick. Let's give Mopey a hand. That must've worn him out."

He had already noticed the Cuban-looking guy in the crowd, lining the cement rail. Yellow shirt, white jacket. The same one Karen had pointed to who'd been sitting at the bar last night. Marta's brother.

Maguire, on the aluminum pole, gave them the double hand-feeding with Bonnie and Pebbles, wondering if Marta's brother was here to give him a message.

And the other Cuban-looking guy with him, why was he along, what, to watch?

Maguire asked the crowd, the little kids, if they wanted to see a mouth-to-mouth feeding. They said, "Yeeeeeeeeees!"

No, he had seen too many like the other Cuban-looking guy. They were bouncers in go-go joints. They hung around sports arenas. Marta's brother looked like he'd been a fighter; the neck, the trace of scar tissue around the eyes. The other Cuban-looking guy was bigger; he could be a lightheavy sparring partner for a good middleweight.

"And that's our Flying Dolphin Show for this afternoon," Maguire said, and told everyone next, to kindly proceed to the Shark Lagoon area. Hooker was doing the color over there today. Maguire's next job, in about twenty minutes, was to announce Brad Allen and then he'd be through. He picked up the bucket of fish sections, looked over at the two guys as he stepped off the platform to the cement deck.

They were waiting. The only ones still up here.

Maguire walked toward the stairway. He heard one of them say, "Just a minute."

And thought, Your ass.

He put the bucket down without breaking stride, moving with purpose but not running yet or looking around, down the stairway to the dim second level, the underwater windows of the tank showing dull-green.

Now run. And if they ran after him, it was absolutely for certain not to deliver a message he wanted to hear. He began running as he heard them on the stairway, his barefeet patting on the cement, their running steps coming after him now, hitting hard, echoing. He ran past the tank windows seeing gray shapes in the water, Bonnie and Pebbles grazing the glass, pacing him as he ran all the way around the circular second level to the stairway again and up to the top deck.

The bucket of fish sections was where he'd left it. Maguire picked it up and stepped back from the open doorway, hearing their steps coming up toward him now, stiffened his arm holding the bucket, let the first one come through to the outside, Marta's brother, and swung the bucket into the face of the other Cuban-looking guy, turning him reeling, took the bucket in both hands, fish pieces falling out, jammed it down over the guy's head and, still holding onto it, ran the bucket, the guy coming with it to the waist-high rail, hitting the cement as Maguire grabbed the guy's legs and threw him into the tank.

Marta's brother stood watching.

Maguire moved to the wire gate in the rail that opened to a small platform on the other side, close to the water, where Hooker would go into the tank with his mask and air hose. Maguire waited, looking from the gate to Marta's brother who was fifteen to twenty feet away.

"What do you want?"

Jesus Diaz said, "This is a warning." He didn't know what else to say. "Keep away from the woman."

Maguire said, "What?" Not sure he heard him right. He looked past the gate to see the other Cuban pulling himself up on the platform. Wet-gray bottlenose heads came out of the water to watch. Maguire waited until the Cuban's hand reached the top of the wire gate, his face appearing, coming up slowly, and slammed a right hook into the face, sending the man back into the tank as the dolphin heads disappeared.

"I'm talking about Missus DiCilia," Jesus said. "Keep away from her or we gonna throw you in that tank for good."

Maguire scowled. His hand hurt something awful. He said to Jesus, "You work for Roland or what?"

Jesus said, "Be smart, uh? Stay away from her."

Or what? Maguire thought. He took two steps toward Jesus, saw the man's hands go behind his back and reappear with a gun, a heavy automatic, Colt or a Browning. The other guy was coming up out of the water again.

Maguire said, "Well, I got to go."

Jesus said, "Don't work too hard."

Maguire went down the stairway holding his sore hand, shaking his head.

12.

"The first thing you better do," Maguire said, "is fire your maid, and anybody else around here. How about the brother?"

"No, he doesn't work for me."

Karen was wearing big round sunglasses and a brown and white striped robe, open. Maguire couldn't see her face, her expression, as she looked at him and then out across the lawn; but he could see her brown legs and firm little belly and the strip of tan material almost covering her breasts. Maguire wore jeans and a shirt over his red Seascape T-shirt. He had come here from work and now, on the patio, he was trying to make Gretchen go away so he could concentrate on Karen.

She said, "I can't believe it. Marta's been here as long as I have. I think she was seventeen when we hired her."

"Give her a reference then," Maguire said. He'd push Gretchen away and she'd come back to him, thinking he was playing.

"I can't just fire her."

"Can you get rid of her for awhile? Send her on an errand."

"She did the grocery shopping yesterday—"

"Tell her you need some Spaghetti-O's, something. We've got to get her out of here."

"For how long?"

"An hour anyway."

Karen got up and went into the house.

Maguire watched her. She didn't seem worried or

upset. She didn't have nervous moves or do anything with her hands. Andre Patterson would try to sign her up.

Maguire had told her about Jesus Diaz and the other one coming to see him, not telling her all of it, but making a point of the warning. That was clear enough, wasn't it? Jesus worked for Roland. If they knew things about Karen that Marta could have observed, then Marta was telling them. And if they knew things Marta couldn't have known, then the house was bugged or there was a tap on the phone. Probably a tap. Karen had said, "Really?" quietly interested. Was she different again? She seemed different every time he saw her.

There was a newspaper on the umbrella table, part of the *Miami Herald,* the "Living Today" section. Maguire reached for it. It wasn't today's "Living Today" though. It was last Sunday's, and he didn't immediately recognize the woman in the photo. Karen DiCilia and a man, her former husband—yes, somewhat familiar to Maguire from newspaper photos years ago—Frank DiCilia. Both dressed up, both wearing dark glasses, coming out of someplace, a doorman standing behind them.

The headline said, WHAT IS KAREN DICILIA'S SECRET? A smaller line, above it, said, WIDOW OF MOBSTER WON'T TALK.

In the Miami paper, taking up the top half of the page. He didn't know how he could have missed it.

The story below, with before-and-after shots of a woman, said, TWENTY-YEAR WAR ON FAT TAPERS OFF IN VICTORY, and maybe Aunt Leona had cut it out of the paper. There were usually things cut out of the *Herald* by the time he got it Sunday evening.

"Widow of Mobster . . ." Jesus, he bet she loved that. The photo with Frank was dated four years ago. She looked the same.

"Why would an attractive forty-year-old widow, comfortably situated, chic, outgoing . . ."

Forty years old?

And that was four years ago.

". . . give up her independence to marry a former

(?) Detroit mob boss relocated in Fort Lauderdale's fashionable Harbor Beach area?"

Maguire's eyes moved down the columns. Background stuff. Formerly Karen Hill. Married to an engineer. Daughter an actress.

"Since Frank DiCilia's death, Karen has become virtually a recluse, seldom venturing out to the fashionable clubs or attending the charitable benefits that used to be de rigueur for her.

"Turn to Page 2D Col. 1"

Maguire turned.

"Woman of Intrigue"

And a current shot of Karen in a pale bikini, hands on her hips, white sunhat and sunglasses, a grainy photo that had been blown up or shot from some distance.

Maguire looked out past the lawn to the seawall, where she might have been standing in the photo.

The hands on hips defiant rather than provocative. The soft hat brim straight across her eyes behind round sunglasses. Nice shot. The slim body somewhat slouched, but in control; yes, with a hint of defiance.

A phrase caught his eye. "The mystery lady of Isla Bahía," and he thought, It's a good thing she doesn't live on Northeast Twenty-ninth Street.

It didn't look as though the reporter, a woman, had learned much about her. There seemed to be more questions than facts. Maguire was still reading the piece when Karen came out.

She said, "Oh," for a moment off guard.

"I didn't know I was with a celebrity," Maguire said. He held the newspaper section aside, looking up at her.

"You didn't?" Karen said. She took the paper from him and folded it into a small square, hiding something thousands of people had already seen.

"That's a nice shot of you in the swimsuit." The same one he was looking at now, the robe hanging open, very thin waist, tight little tummy curving into the tan panties that crossed her loins in a straight line. Maguire moved in the canvas chair, reseating himself.

"It was taken here, wasn't it?"

"From a boat. I didn't know it was a news photographer."

"They're starting to move in on you."

She looked at him, but didn't say anything. Her expression almost the same as the one in the photo.

"The woman that wrote it," Maguire said, "why didn't you tell her what's going on?"

"How could I do that?"

"Why not? Get it out in the open."

"Don't you think I'd look a little stupid? The dumb widow involved in some Sicilian oath."

"Well, you're not dumb and it *is* happening, isn't it? What I'm thinking, you expose Roland and maybe he'll go away."

"And expose Karen DiCilia," Karen said. "Would you like to read about yourself, involved in something like this, in a newspaper?"

"I don't know," Maguire said, "if I thought it would do the job."

"I have to handle Roland," Karen said, "if Ed Grossi doesn't." She folded the newspaper section again and shoved it into the pocket of her robe. "I gave Marta the evening off."

"Good," Maguire said.

"She didn't want to go." Karen was watching him now from behind her sunglasses. "I told her we wanted to be alone. It doesn't matter now what she thinks, does it?"

"It never did," Maguire said.

He located the telephone line coming in from the street, through the mangrove trees, to the house, and pointed to the piece of metal clamped to the line, an infinity transmitter. A second line ran from the terminal point at the house to a corner window and entered Marta's room between the brick and the window casing.

In the room itself the line led to a voltage-activated recorder beneath Marta's bed. Maguire explained it—

part of an accumulation of knowledge picked up along the way to nowhere; though sometimes bits and pieces came in handy.

"The telephone rings, the voltage on the line automatically turns on the cassette, and the phone conversation is recorded on a cartridge tape. Marta gives the tape to her brother or Roland and they know who you talk to, where you're going—I guess they learn all they need to know."

Karen didn't say anything. She stared at the recorder, her words in there, the sound of her voice contained within the flat cartridge, with its window and two round holes. Telling what?

"You want to give Roland a message?" Maguire flicked a switch on and off.

Still she didn't say anything.

"Get rid of Marta," Maguire said.

"Or keep her. Let them listen," Karen said. "Which is better, if Roland finds out we know about it or if he doesn't?"

"That went through my mind," Maguire said. "I let it go."

Karen looked up from the recorder. "It might be to our advantage."

"We talk," Maguire said. "I phoned—that's how they knew we were meeting the other night."

"But what do they learn, really? We could use some kind of code."

She was serious, taking off her sunglasses now, her eyes quietly alive.

"The question is, what did Roland hear before," Maguire said. "Something he might've learned that turned him on, you might say, to go independent."

"What do you mean, turned him on?"

"Like money," Maguire said. He hesitated, then took a chance. "Maybe he heard you tell somebody you keep money in the house." She was staring at him now, and he looked down at the recorder again, fingering the different switches. "It's just a thought. Or he heard you talking to your accountant, your banker, somebody like that. It'd be a way of finding out what you're worth."

"Maybe he's not the only one who's interested," Karen said.

"No, your maid, her brother—"

"What do you think I'm worth?" Karen said.

"I don't know, three million, thirty million," Maguire said. "You get into those figures, I don't see much difference. But how does he get his hands on it unless it's sitting there. You're not gonna write him a check."

"He hasn't asked for anything."

"No, but he's leading up to something. We're pretty sure of that."

"You haven't asked for anything either," Karen said.

"What am I, the help? You hiring me?"

"That's not an answer," Karen said.

"Why don't I go home and get dressed," Maguire said. "We'll go out, have dinner, hold hands, look at each other. You can tell me what you want, and I'll tell you what I want. How's that sound?"

"I'll tell you right now what I want," Karen said.

Maguire picked up a pizza on the way home (Were they ever going to go out and have dinner together?), took off his shirt, put a cold beer on the table, and began eating, starving.

There were three rattling knocks on the front-door jalousie. Lesley came in still wearing her white shorts, no shoes, and a striped tanktop. She said, "I just got in, too; I was out all evening. Hey, can I have a piece?"

"Help yourself."

"What kind is it?"

"Pepperoni, onions, cheese, a few other things."

"Yuk, anchovies."

Like they were worms. Lesley being sensitive, delicate. He wondered when she'd ask about the car, the silver-gray Mercedes 450 SEL parked in front. She took dainty bites, holding an open palm beneath the wedge, bending over the table to give him a shot of her breasts hanging free in the tanktop.

"You still have Sunday's paper?"

"How should I know?"

"Aunt Leona keeps newspapers, doesn't she? Gives them to some charity drive?"

"She sells them. She's so goddamn money-hungry. Where you going?"

"I'll be right back."

Maguire went in through the manager's apartment, past Leona asleep in her Barcalounger, with a TV movie on, to the utility room off the kitchen. There were several weeks of newspapers stacked against the wall. He began looking through the first pile and there it was, last Sunday's edition of the *Herald,* finding it right away. Sometimes that happened. He pulled out the "Living Today" section, glancing at Karen and Frank DiCilia, then took the sports section, too, and slipped "Living Today" in behind the sports pages.

Lesley was sitting now, her chair turned away from the table, one foot on the seat, a tan expanse of inner thigh facing him. A lot of flesh there.

"Why're you so interested in the paper?"

"There's a story on the Tigers I missed."

"I think baseball's boring. Nothing ever happens."

Maguire was eating. He didn't care what Lesley thought. He wondered, though, how she'd get around to the car.

She said, "Brad's really pissed at you, you know it?"

"Why?"

"You were supposed to stay after and work with Bubbles."

It sounded like she was talking about school.

"I forgot," Maguire said. He'd left without looking back, not wanting to see the two Cubans again.

"Brad saw you take off in the car. He goes, 'Jesus Christ, where'd he get that, steal it?' "

That was how she did it, indirectly. Maguire worked his way through another pizza wedge, not giving her any help.

"Brad goes, 'He didn't have it yesterday. He must've got it last night.' "

Maguire drank some of the cold beer: really good with the salty achovy taste.

" 'Somebody must've loaned it to him.' Then he goes, 'But who would he know that owns a fucking Mercedes?' "

"I bet you said that, not Brad," Maguire said.

"I might've. Somebody said it."

"It's a friend of mine's," Maguire said. "I'm using it while he's out of town."

"Well, let's go someplace in it."

"I'm not allowed to take passengers. He's afraid it'll get messed up."

"You big shit, you're just saying that."

"It's the truth."

"Who's is it?"

"Guy by the name of Andre Patterson."

"The one you were talking to on the phone?"

Talking *about* on the phone to Andre's wife, but it didn't matter. "Right. He went on a vacation." Christ, 20 to life. He should write to Andre, tell him how things were going. He wanted to read the newspaper story again and look at the picture of Karen on the seawall.

"How would he know the difference?" Lesley said. "I mean just me, not a lot of people."

"Maybe," Maguire said. "You want some more?"

"No . . . I feel like—" She gave him a sly look. "You know how I feel?"

"How?"

"Horny. Isn't that funny? I don't know why." She looked over at the bed. "You want to lie down, see what happens?"

"Your feet are dirty," Maguire said.

"My *feet?*"

"Actually I'm awful tired. You mind?"

"Jesus Christ," Lesley said, getting up. "You have a headache, too?"

"No, but I don't feel too good. I think maybe the pizza." He said, "Why don't you catch me some other time, okay?"

"Why don't you catch this," Lesley said, giving him the finger and slammed the jalousie door, rattling the frosted-glass louvers.

There were times, yes, when he didn't mind dirty feet. Or, there had been times. But going from one to the other, from the woman to the girl, he couldn't imagine ever having to try and compare them. Hearing Lesley's voice, "Brad's really pissed at you." Serious. A crisis because he'd forgotten to stay after closing to work with the young dolphin. "Brad goes, 'What'd he do, steal it?' " Brad and Lesley, the whole setup, like a summer camp. Then hearing Karen's voice:

"What do you think I'm worth?"

Karen's voice:

"I'll tell you right now what I want."

Not putting it on, trying to act sultry, but straight. Looking at him without the sunglasses. "I'll tell you right now what I want."

She wanted it, too. She had said the first time, "I could hardly wait." This time was like the first time multiplied, more of it, more free and easy with each other, fooling with each other in that big broken-down bed, then getting into it, picking it up, beginning to race, feeling the rush. It was as different as day and night, the girl and the woman. The girl okay, very good in fact, but predictable: the same person all the way, making little put-on sounds—"Oh, oh, oh, don't stop now, God, don't ever stop"—she must've read somewhere and decided that was how you made the guy feel good. The woman, the forty-four-year-old woman didn't fake anything. She watched him with a soft, slightly smiling look that was natural. She moved her hands all over him, everywhere, which the girl never did—as though the girl was supposed to get it and not give unless she gave as a special favor; the girl very open and, quote, together, saying, "You want to fuck?" if she felt like it; except that it had no bearing on how she was in bed—the girl not aware of the two of them the way the forty-four-year-old woman was.

The woman in the photograph. The lady in the million dollar home. The lady. That was the key maybe. The lady, with a poise and quiet tone, easing out of the role as they moved over and around each other on the bed, not being tricky about it but natural, touching, entering the special place of the slim, good-looking lady, moving in and owning the place for awhile, right there tight in the place, and the lady trying to keep him, hold onto him there. Yes, there. Now that was different. That was being as close to someone as you could get without completely disappearing into the person, gone. Man. To look forward to that for another—how many years? Wondering if it was a consideration, a possibility. Maybe not. But at least feeling close enough to be able to say, "They got your age wrong in the paper." Smiling.

"They got a number of things wrong," Karen said, "including the way it was written."

"All the questions. It was like a quiz." Kissing her shoulder, her neck, feeling it moist. "I don't care how old you are . . . we are. What difference does it make?"

"None that I can think of," Karen said.

Her tone was all right, but what did it mean? *None,* because the way they felt, it didn't matter? Or *none,* because nothing was going to come of this anyway?

"I'm almost forty," Maguire said. "It's just another number. Forty, that's all."

"Then why are you talking about it?" Karen said.

They went downstairs and sat in the living room, with drinks Karen made at the built-in marble bar. Maguire checked the room for hidden mikes planted behind figurines and paintings or in the white sofa and easy chairs. They talked about Roland, what he might ask for, wondering if they could get him to ask for it over the phone, make an extortion demand and hook him with his own device. Which wasn't likely. Sometime, Karen said, she'd like him to look at the antiques and art objects and tell her what they were worth. Maguire was ready to do it now, but they went outside instead, all the way out to the seawall. They stood looking at tinted points of light in the homes across the channel, at cold reflections in the water. He thought of the photo again that had been taken here, Karen standing with hands on hips, legs somewhat apart, sunhat and sunglasses—the slim, good-looking woman who was close to him, in a skirt now, barefoot.

He liked skirts. He liked the idea of lifting up a skirt, something from his boyhood, something you did with girls. She moved against him when he began to kiss her. She let herself be lowered to the grass where he began to bring her skirt up to her hips and put his hand under it.

Gretchen came out and hopped around them, sniffing their legs. Maguire told the dog to get the hell out of there.

Sitting on the patio, another drink; were they going to go out to eat or not? It was strange the way she brought up the question of the dog, surprising him, asking him why he wasn't nice to Gretchen.

He said, "What do you mean I'm not nice to her? What do you say to a dog that's not nice?"

She said, "You ignore her. Until tonight you only said one word to her, the first time you came here, you told her to relax."

"Well, that was nice," Maguire said. "What do I want to talk to a dog for? I talk to dolphins all day, and I don't ordinarily, you're right, talk to animals at all. I don't have that much to say to them."

She said, "You know who's nice to Gretchen?"

He said, "I'll talk to the dog when I have time. I'll be very happy to."

"Roland," Karen said. "He can't keep his hands off her."

Maguire said, "Well, I'd keep an eye on him if I were you."

He said that, and they were friends again. The strange part was feeling a little tension between them over the dog. Or else he imagined it.

No, the dog wasn't a problem. What mattered was, they always got back to Roland.

He said to her, "I guess I'm gonna have to meet him, aren't I?" A few moments later he said, "I don't see you having conversations with the dog."

13.

The reason Roland served the six months at Lake Butler:

Dade County Criminal Division had charged Jimmy Capotorto with three counts second degree and one count first degree murder: the victims being the three employees who died in the Coral Gables Discount Mart fire and the star witness who died of gunshot wounds in the parking lot of the VA Hospital. Dade County *knew*, circumstantially, Coral Gables Discount had borrowed shylock money from Jimmy Cap. They had the written testimony of the star witness, the former Coral Gables Discount owner, that described how Jimmy Cap had taken over management of the company and had decided to liquidate. They lost their star witness in the VA Hospital parking lot, on Eighteenth Street Road. But they now had a second star witness who described Jimmy Cap and revealed the license number of his two-tone red and white Sedan d'Ville pulling out of the lot moments following the sound of several gunshots; this within two blocks of the Dade County Public Safety Department offices. Jimmy Cap's lawyer pointed out that the first star witness was a drug addict and had gone to the VA Hospital parking lot to purchase stolen morphine to relieve his tensions. The second star witness, however, was a one-legged ex-Marine who had come out of the hospital after visiting one of his buddies. He said on the witness stand, pointing to Jimmy Capotorto, "Yes sir, that's him."

Jimmy Cap's lawyer put Roland Crowe on the stand, and Roland said Jimmy Cap had spent the evening with him visiting a Cuban lady out on Beaver Road off the Tamiami Trail. The Cuban lady was waiting to go on next if they needed her.

The state's prosecutor hammered away at Roland's credibility, bringing out the fact Roland himself had served eight years in Raford for second degree murder —objected to and sustained, but there it was—then asked Roland if he had spoken to their witness, the ex-Marine, out in the hall. Roland said, "No sir." The prosecutor said hadn't he, Roland, said to the ex-Marine, "You only got one leg now. How'd you like to keep talking and go for none?" Roland said if the Marine had said that, then the Marine was a fucking liar. The judge warned Roland his language would not be tolerated. The prosecutor kept at Roland, trying to hook him. But Roland remained cool. He said to the state's prosecutor, "What you say, sir, is your opinion. The only thing is, opinions're like assholes, everybody's got one."

Roland was sentenced to a year and a day for contempt, reduced to six months following an appeal. But he had stared long enough at that one-legged Marine, who finally said maybe he'd been mistaken about his testimony.

Jimmy Cap talked about it all the time, describing Roland on the witness stand, even describing Roland to Roland himself, the way the gator had fucked their minds around with his you-all bullshit and had actually dis*tract*ed them from the reason they were in court. Jimmy Cap, at one point, had said to Roland, "Hey, I owe you six months."

When Roland came to see Jimmy Cap, at his office in the Dorado Management suite, Jimmy Cap said, "Buddy"—meaning it—"what can I do for you?"

"I was supposed to see Ed," Roland said, "but I guess he's out of town."

"So talk to Vivian."

"Vivian's out too."

"Is it important?"

"He'll chew my ass cuz I can't find him."

"When they're both away," Jimmy Cap said, "they're shacked up at Vivian's for a couple of days. Ed tells Clara he's gone to Pittsburgh or some fucking place, they're up in Keystone."

"Yeah?" Roland grinned, tilted up his Ox Bow and sat down. "That reminds me. The company manages a condo up in Boca, don't it?"

"Oceana," Jimmy Cap said.

"And Frank DiCilia had a place there he used, if I ain't mistaken?"

"That's right."

"But I don't imagine anybody's using it much no more. I know the lady ain't cuz I'm the one watching her. You know about that?"

"Jesus," Jimmy Cap said, "that's a weird setup. Ed told me something about it, I said, Jesus Christ, we back in the fucking Sicilian Mountains or Miami, Florida? We got better things to do. She's not a bad-looking broad either, you know it?"

"Look but don't touch," Roland said. "I got one firmer and younger up in Boca just dying for it. But this problem, see, she's a waitress at a place up there? And she's married. She can get out of the house only maybe a couple hours in the evening; but I don't have no place to take her up there. You follow me? I mean a nice place, to impress her a little bit."

Jimmy Cap said, "So you're thinking of Frank's apartment."

"If it's sitting there going to waste," Roland said. "I remember I took a piss in there once, it had this great big bathtub you walked up some steps to get in."

"Clean the little waitress up first," Jimmy Cap said. "Sure, I'll get you a key anytime you want."

"Now'd be fine," Roland said. He waited a moment. "Oh, hey, you got Vivian's private number up there in Keystone?"

"Is it important?"

"Life or death situation," Roland said. He grinned, but he meant it.

Maguire said, "I'm gonna make a phone call, that's all. I'll be right there."

Brad Allen said, "You come to my office right now or you're out of a job."

The camp director. The school principal. Tell him what to do with the job.

Maguire watched him walking away. Pretty soon, he thought. He followed Brad to the office beneath the grandstand, ten by twelve, with a wooden desk, one chair, four cement walls covered with photos of Brad Allen and dolphins—Brad & Pepper, Brad & Dixie, Brad & Bonnie—Brad feeding, patting, kissing, presenting, admonishing, cajoling dozens of different one-name dolphins that, to Maguire, all looked like the same one.

Brad, seated, looking up at Maguire standing at parade rest, said, "All right, here's the new routine. You ready?"

"I'm ready," Maguire said.

"Beginning of the Flying Dolphin Show, most of the people've just come in. Right?"

"Right."

"You say, 'Anybody notice that lion out there by the main entrance?' " Brad's tone becoming an effortless drawl.

Jesus Christ, Maguire thought.

" 'We got Leo—that's the lion's name—to keep out undesirables, anybody that might come in and cause trouble. But the trouble is, the lion's asleep all the time. Never moves. That's why you might not've noticed him.' Then you say, 'Leo did cause a problem, though, one time, back when, for some reason, our porpoises were all getting sick and dying on us. Well, this fella came along and said, "What you got to do is feed your porpoises seagull meat, and I guarantee they'll live forever." He said he'd supply it, too. Well, we'd try anything, so we told him okay, bring some gull meat. Well, the next day he's walking in with it, stepping over Leo, when all of a sudden about a dozen cops jumped out and arrested him. And you know what for?' You wait then, make sure you've got everybody's attention. Then you say, 'He was arrested for transporting gulls over the staid lion for immortal porpoises.' " Brad Allen grinned. "Huh? What do you think?"

"Can I use your phone?" Maguire said.

"Karen, how are you?"

"Who is this?"

"You know who it is."

"Let me see. Is it Howard?"

"Come on—"

"Don't you know when I'm kidding?"

"Well, I thought I had a sense of humor, but I think it was just ruined for good. Like pouring sugar in a gas tank."

"Where are you?"

"I'm at work. Listen, let's meet tonight."

There was a silence. Karen wondering what to say.

"At the Yankee Clipper. No, I'll try to pick you up about eight, then we'll go there. Okay?"

Tentatively, "Okay." A pause. "Are you sure?"

"Yeah, there's somebody I want to see. So wait for me to pick you up."

"I understand," Karen said.

Jesus Diaz had taken Lionel Oliva to Abbey Hospital to get thirteen stitches in his head and four inside his lower lip. They were in the Centro Vasco the next day, in the afternoon, Jesus having something to eat, Lionel Oliva drinking beer, holding it against the swollen cut in his mouth, when Roland came in. Roland said, "What's the matter with him?"

"He hit his head," Jesus said.

"I want you to pick up the tape after supper and drop it off," Roland said.

Jesus looked up at Roland and said, "I'm going to Cuba."

"What d'ya mean you're going to Cuba? Shit, nobody goes down there. It's against the law."

Jesus had, only this moment, thought of Cuba. If he wasn't going there he'd go someplace else. "You can go there now," he said. "I got to see my mother. She's dying."

"Well, shit," Roland said, "I got things going on, I got to go up to Hallandale—" Roland was frowning; he didn't like this. "When you coming back?"

"I don't know," Jesus said. "I have to wait to see if she dies."

"Well, listen, you pick up the tape and drop it off 'fore you go to Cuba. Don't forget, either." Roland turned and went toward the front of the quiet, nearly empty restaurant.

"Where did he get that suit?" Lionel Oliva said, not moving his mouth. "It makes you close your eyes."

Jesus Diaz was still watching Roland, the hat, the high round shoulders, the light behind him as he moved toward the front entrance.

"I'd like to be able to hit him," Jesus said. "I would, you know it? If I could reach him."

"When you going to Cuba?" Lionel Oliva said.

"Fuck Cuba," Jesus said. "Man, I'd like to hit him, one time. I think I'd like a Tom Collins, too."

Roland liked Arnold Rapp's balcony view a whole lot more than his own. You could look straight down on the swimming pool and some palm trees or turn your head a notch and there was the Atlantic Ocean. It didn't make sense. Here was Arnold, about to have a nervous breakdown, with the good view. Whereas Roland, who had the world by the giggy at the present time, had a piss-poor view of the ocean down a street and between some apartments.

He said to Arnold, "You don't get outside enough. Look at you."

"*Look* at me?" Arnold said. "How'm I gonna get outside, I'm on the fucking telephone all day. Now, you know what I gotta do now? Borrow money, for Christ sake, a hundred grand, guy I know in New York—if he was here I'd kiss him, shit, I'd blow him, he says he's gonna come through. That's what I have to do, get deeper in hock so I can buy time to put together some deals, I ought to go outside."

"You got this week's?" Roland said.

"What're you talking about this week's? I don't owe you till Friday."

"Couple of days, what's the difference?"

"You kidding? Almost eight grand a day, man; it makes all the fucking difference in the world."

"Ed don't think you're gonna pay it."

"He doesn't, huh."

"He thinks you're gonna get on a aeroplane one of these days," Roland said. "He thinks we ought to settle up. So he said go on see Arnie, get it done."

"Get what done? Jesus Christ, now wait a minute—"

Roland reached inside his suitcoat and brought out a .45 caliber Smith & Wesson revolver with a six and one-half inch barrel, one of the guns he kept stored for this kind of work.

"Now come on—Jesus, put it away."

Extended, pointed at Arnold sitting on the couch, the big Smith covered Arnold's face and half his body. Roland reached down to the easy chair next to him and picked up a satin pillow. He held it in front of the muzzle, showing Arnold how he was going to do it as he moved toward him, the poor little guy pressing himself against the couch, nowhere to go, looking like he was about to cry.

"I'm gonna pay you. Man, I'm *pay*ing you, haven't I been paying? I got some money now you can have."

"Shut your eyes, Arnie." Roland took the pillow away so Arnie could look into the .45 muzzle that was like a tunnel coming toward his face. "Close your little eyes, go seepy-bye."

Those eyes wild, frantic, the gun right there in his face.

"Ready?" Roland said. "Close 'em tight."

Arnold grabbed the barrel, wrenching it, twisting, rolling across the satin couch. Roland yelled out something, his finger caught in the trigger guard, then grabbing the finger as it came free, holding it tight, the finger hurting something awful, and there was Arnold aiming the gun at him now, pointing it directly at his chest, Arnold closing his eyes, the dumb son of a bitch, as he held the Smith in both hands and pulled the trigger.

Click.

Pulled it again.

Click.

And again and again.

Click, click.

Roland grinned.

Arnold hunched over and started to cry.

Roland took the gun from him, lifting it between thumb and two fingers by the checkered walnut grip and slipped it back into the inside pocket of his suit jacket. He patted Arnold on the shoulder.

"It ain't your day, is it, Arnie? Come on out on the balcony."

Arnold pulled away from him, his mouth ugly the way he was crying without making much of a sound.

"You dink, I ain't gonna throw you off. We're gonna sit out in the air while I tell you how you can get born again."

"I don't see why I can't meet him someplace here," Arnold said. He was sighing, but starting to breathe normally again.

Poor little fella, his nose wet and snotty. Roland handed him a red bandana handkerchief.

"You got Drug Enforcement on your ass, you dink.

Ed ain't gonna chance being seen with you around here."

"I don't see why Detroit."

"Arnie, I don't give a shit if you see it or not. That's where Ed says he'll meet you."

"When?"

"Tomorrow, maybe the day after. You go to the hotel there at the Detroit airport and wait for a call. Ed'll get in touch with you."

"Yeah, but when?"

"When he feels like it, you dink." Shit, maybe he ought to forget the whole thing and throw the dink off the balcony.

"Then what?"

"Then you meet someplace, you tell him your deal."

"What deal?"

"Jesus Christ, you told me to get Ed to bank a couple of more trips, and he could take it all. Didn't you tell me that?"

"Yeah, right. I wasn't sure."

"Listen, Ace, I'm standing here in the middle with my pecker hanging out. You better be sure you got a deal to make him."

"Don't worry about it."

Roland liked that tone of confidence coming back into Arnold's voice, the dumb shithead. He brought a folded Delta Airlines envelope out of his side pocket and handed it to Arnold.

"This here's your flight. Tomorrow noon. You'll be driving out to the airport in your Jaguar, huh? License ARN-268?"

"I'll probably take a cab."

"Drive," Roland said, "case somebody wants to follow you, see that you go to the airport and not take off for the big swamp."

"Something's funny," Arnold said.

"Okay," Roland said, "let's forget the whole thing, asshole. I'll see you in two days for the vig. I'll see you next week and the week after—"

"It's just a little funny," Arnold said. "I mean it isn't *that* funny. Not nearly as funny as that shit you pulled with the gun. You got a very weird sense of humor, if you don't mind my saying."

"No, I don't mind," Roland said. "We were just having us some fun, weren't we?"

14.

Marta's brother, Jesus, came for the cassette tape a little after seven o'clock, while Mrs. DiCilia was upstairs. He said this was the last time. No more.

Marta asked him if he had been drinking. He said yes, with Lionel Oliva. He said, Why are we doing this? It wasn't a question. Why should we make life difficult for the woman? What has she done to us? Why should we want to deceive her? Still not asking questions. Marta listened. No more, Jesus said. You're drunk, Marta said. Jesus said, How does that change it? No more. Doing this for Roland. How can a man work for Roland and live with himself? Still not a question. Marta said, All I do is hand you this. Nothing more. Jesus said, *No* more! You feel the same way I feel. (Which was true.) So no more. I'm leaving. Marta said, But if I leave—Jesus said, I leave to be away from Roland. You don't have to leave. Talk to the woman. Help her for a change. Marta said, Where are you going? Cuba, Jesus said. Then why give him this one? Marta said. Because when I go to see him and give it to him, Jesus said, I may have the nerve to shoot him. Or I may not. But I think I'm going to Cuba.

Then the one named Maguire came in Mrs. DiCilia's car at five minutes to eight.

Marta thought Mrs. DiCilia was going out with him, but they spoke outside for a few minutes and then the one named Maguire drove away. Mrs. DiCilia returned to the house and went up to the room that had been Mr. DiCilia's office, next to the master bedroom. Mrs. DiCilia had gone to the public library today—

she had told Marta—for several hours, then had returned to spend most of the day in the room.

Marta remained in her own room for nearly an hour, telling herself it wasn't wrong to record Mrs. DiCilia's telephone calls; it was for the woman's protection—which is what they had told her—to keep bad men away from her. But if the men who were supposed to be protecting her were worse than the ones they were keeping away— If she *knew* this— Yes, then she could say to Mrs. DiCilia she had just found it out or realized it. Not confessing, but revealing a discovery. There was a great difference. For then Mrs. DiCilia would trust her and have no reason to fire her. Marta wanted to help Mrs. DiCilia. But she first wanted to keep her job.

She went upstairs to the office-room, where Mrs. DiCilia sat at the desk holding the telephone and a pair of scissors.

There was something different about the room. The white walls were bare. The framed photographs of Mr. DiCilia and other men—Mr. DiCilia shaking hands with them or standing smiling with them—were gone. They had been taken down.

Marta waited.

Mrs. DiCilia was speaking to someone named Clara, saying all right, she'd phone him the day after tomorrow, then.

There were newspapers and pieces cut from newspapers covering the surface of the desk, pictures out of the paper, pictures out of magazines, that seemed to be of Mrs. DiCilia.

Mrs. DiCilia was asking if Clara had the phone number of Vivian Arzola.

Marta, looking at the pictures on the desk and thinking, It's being recorded. The telephone. Roland will come for the tape and—what would she tell him?

There were small snapshots in black and white on the desk, and newspaper pictures of another woman, not Mrs. DiCilia, that had been machine-copied and looked marked and faded.

Mrs. DiCilia was saying all right, she'd try to call Vivian at the office again, and thanked the one named Clara.

Mrs. DiCilia hung up the telephone, looking at Marta. "Yes?"

"I have something I want to tell you please," Marta said.

"Where's a cowboy get a hat like that?"

Roland turned his head to look at Maguire on the bar stool next to him. He said, "Right in downtown Miami. There's a store there sells range clothes."

"Like western attire," Maguire said. "I believe if I'm not mistaken it's the Ox Bow model." As advertised in the window of Bill Bullock's in Aspen.

"You're right," Roland said, touching the curved brim and looking at Maguire again, a man who knew hats.

"But you didn't get that suit there," Maguire said.

"No, the suit was made for me over in the Republic of China," Roland said.

Maguire shook his head. "No shit."

"Yeah, over in Taiwan. It cost you some money, but if you're willing to pay—"

"I know what you mean."

"—then you got yourself a suit of clothes." Roland's chin rested on his shoulder, looking at Maguire. "I bet I know where you're from. Out west."

"How'd you know?" Maguire said, giving it just a little down-home accent.

"I can tell. Where you think I'm from?"

"Well, I was gonna say out west, too," Maguire said. "I don't know. Let me see—Vegas?"

Roland straightened around, looking down the bar at the display of bottles and the portholes full of illuminated water. "Bartender, give us a couple more here, if you will please." Then to Maguire, "What're you drinking?"

"Rum," Maguire said.

"One Caribbean piss," Roland said to the bartender,

"one Wild Turkey. Las Vegas, huh? Shit no, I'm from right here in Florida."

"Lemme see," Maguire said, "you a cattle rancher? Those brahmans with the humps?"

"Naw, I was in cement, land development. Before that I was a hunting-fishing guide over in Big Cypress. Take these dinks out don't know shit, one end of a air boat from the other."

"Over by Miccosukee I bet," Maguire said.

"Near, but more west, by Turner River."

"I drove through there one time," Maguire said, "I stopped at this place on the Tamiami for a cup of coffee?"

"Yeah."

"Little restaurant out there all by itself. This woman about thirty-five, nice looking, serves me the coffee and then she sits down in a chair right in the middle of the floor, I'm sitting at the counter?"

"Yeah."

"She says, 'I love animals. It tears me up when one gets run over by a car.' She says, 'I love cowbirds the most. They have the prettiest eyes.' With this dreamy look on her face, sitting out in the middle of the floor. She says, 'Their little heads go back and forth like this'—she shows me how they go—'pecking away; they'll peck at a great big horsefly.' "

"That's right," Roland said, "they will."

"She's sitting there—I said to her, 'You all by yourself?' She says, 'Yes, I am.' I said, 'You live here?' She says, 'Yes, I do.' I said, 'You want to go back to the bedroom?' She says, 'I don't care.' "

Roland hit the edge of the bar with his big hand. "Yeah, shit, I know where that's at."

"We go back there," Maguire said, "she never says a word all the time we're doing it. We get dressed, come back out, she pours me another cup of coffee and sits down in that same chair again in the middle of the floor?"

"Yeah."

"Hasn't said a word in about twenty minutes now."

"I know."

"She says, 'We found a little parrot was hit by a car once. We nursed it, we got it well again and kept it in the bathroom so it'd be warm. But it drowned in the commode.' "

Roland, shaking his head, said, "Je-sus, I know her and about a hunnert just like her." He opened his eyes and put on a blank expression, turning his head to look around slowly and drawled in a high voice, 'Yeah, I was down to Mon-roe Station, les see, 'bout five years ago for a catfish supper.' Fucking place's a mile and a half down the road. Man, I had to get out of there 'fore I got covered over with moss."

"It ain't the Gold Coast," Maguire said, "nor afford you the opportunities, does it?"

"Make thirty-five hundred a year in the swamp you're big stuff. Over here you turn that up every week or so and sleep in on Saturday."

"I guess if you know what you're doing," Maguire said.

"And got hair on your balls," Roland said. "Right now I'm lining up a deal—when it comes off I'm gonna be set for life as long as I live."

"What is it, land?"

"Land, you could say that," Roland said. "Land, a house, a trust fund." Roland looked over his shoulder, studying the diners at the tables.

Maguire had a close look at the man's creased rawhide face, and it made him feel tired to imagine trying to hit that face and hurt it. Like kicking an alligator. The way to do it, have a friend waiting outside in the car. Start bad-mouthing Roland till he says come on, step outside. Go out in the parking lot and square off, get Roland turned the right way and then the friend guns the car and drives it over Roland, hard.

He said, "You meeting somebody?"

"Yeah, some people I'm suppose to see," Roland said. "There's this dink giving me a bad time. But if they don't come real quick, I'm going."

It was getting too close. "I'm going myself," Maguire said. " 'Less I can buy you a drink." He was becoming anxious to get out of here.

"Well, one more," Roland said, and squared around to the bar. Looking at the portholes, the illuminated green water, he started to grin. "You know what'd be good? Pop one of them windows. See all that swimming pool water come pouring in here"—grinning, enjoying the idea—"People jumping up, trying to get out, shit, the water pouring out all over their dinner."

"Yeah, that'd be good," Maguire said. "Get everybody's dinner all wet."

15.

When the phone rang, Vivian looked at Ed Grossi. Ed had her private number. Jimmy Cap had her number. Her mother in Homestead had it. Ed's lawyer—

Grossi heard her say on the phone, after she had answered in a hesitant voice and spoke to whoever it was for a moment, "What? . . . What're you talking about? I never gave it to you . . . I did not."

Tough lady. Very soft and good to him but a tough lady to keep between him and other people. Twelve years she had worked for him: in the beginning somebody to go to bed with, good-looking young Cuban broad; but too intelligent to remain only a piece of ass. More intelligent, basically, than himself or anyone in the organization; but a little weak in self-confidence because she had been a migrant farmworker and was sometimes intimidated by people with loud voices. Something she had to learn: Loudness did not mean strength or power. Though she could be loud herself sometimes and it seemed to work.

He liked to come here and be alone with Vivian for a few days at a time. Do some thinking. Wear flowered shirts and Bermuda shorts. Try investment ideas on her. Tell her things about his past life he had never told anyone, certainly not his wife, Clara. Go to bed with Vivian. Eat fried bananas. Smoke dope with her, which he never did anywhere else but here. Twelve years only. And yet thinking of his life before Vivian seemed a long time ago, or like looking back at another person named Ed Grossi.

She brought the phone to him, where he sat, in his

favorite deep chair, his thin bare legs extending to the matching ottoman.

"It's Roland."

Seeing her clouded expression, then hearing Roland's sunny voice: "Ed, hey, I hope I ain't taking you away from anything, partner, but I got a little problem come up."

Presenting a problem, but making it sound like it was nothing. Then becoming more serious, with a sound almost of pain, goddarn, not knowing how to handle it and wanting Ed to help him out if he wasn't too busy and could get away for awhile.

Vivian waited, not sitting down, trying to read Ed's expression, which told her nothing, and learn something from his brief words, questions. Something about Karen DiCilia. She took the phone from him when finally he said, "All right, I'll be there," and hung up.

"Be where?" Vivian said.

"Boca. DiCilia's apartment."

"He told me I gave him this number," Vivian said. "I didn't. I know I didn't give it to him. What's he doing there?"

"He says Karen was drunk, talking loud to some reporter, starting to make a scene. So he took her to the apartment."

"Why? Wait a minute." Vivian put the phone on the floor as she sat down on the edge of the ottoman. "Where was this, in Boca?"

"He says in a restaurant. Roland followed her—it looked like she was meeting someone, this woman he finds out is a newspaper reporter or a writer, something like that."

"Yes?"

"But he thinks Karen was already drunk before she got there."

"She drinks much?"

"I don't know, maybe."

"Call her at home," Vivian said.

"What do you mean, call her? She's at the apartment."

"How do you know for sure?"

"I heard her voice. Roland said, 'Just a minute. I heard her say something.' Then Roland said she was sick and went in the bathroom."

Vivian said, "What restaurant was it?"

"He didn't say."

"You're getting old."

Grossi looked at her without saying anything.

"I'm sorry," Vivian said. "Let's call him back and find out the restaurant."

"Why?"

"Call and see if her car's there. If he says he drove her to the apartment. Why there? Why not home?"

"He says the woman reporter would probably go there. He says Karen is going to tell her everything if I don't speak to her first, Vivian. Christ, the bullshit things we get into."

"Let's call him back," Vivian said.

"It's an unlisted number. I don't know what it is." Ed Grossi pulled himself out of the chair and went into the bedroom.

"I can go to the office and get it," Vivian called after him. "Forty minutes."

After a moment Grossi appeared in the bedroom door without his Bermudas now, in striped undershorts. "You can drive me."

"Call her home," Vivian said. "See if she went to Boca."

Grossi was patient with Vivian because he understood her. "I heard her voice on the phone. She's at the apartment, we're going to the apartment. Okay?"

"I didn't give him this number," Vivian said. "I know goddamn well I never gave it to him."

If Ed or Vivian called back, Roland would say, "Just a minute," and put his hand over the phone. Then he'd say, "Shit, now she's passed out."

Or he'd turn his tape recorder on again and give them one of the snatches of Karen's voice he'd pulled off of yesterday's cassette and rerecorded, Karen talking to the newspaper lady who'd called.

Roland punched the recorder to hear it again.

"Why do you keep asking me that if you know what I'm going to say? Think of something else."

Roland would say, first, "Mrs. DiCilia, will you talk to Mr. Grossi, please?"

Then punch the recorder and hold the phone toward it.

"Why do you keep asking me that if you know what I'm going to say?"

Maybe cut it right there. Then say to them, Now she won't talk to nobody. You better come see if you can handle her.

Roland liked this Oceana setup. All modern, bigger than Arnold's place, top-floor view and that deep, square-cut bathtub in there. He just might at that run into a nice cocktail waitress. Bring her up here when he wasn't busy with Karen. Or bring her when he was. That bathtub'd hold three easy.

Roland went over to the closet by the front door, where he'd hung his suit jacket. He lifted the big .45 Smith out of the inside pocket and laid it on the hat shelf of the closet, against the back wall. He left the suitcoat hanging in there, but kept his Ox Bow straw on, resetting it loose, straight over his eyes trooper-fashion. People would ask him, "You ever take your hat off?" He'd say, "Let's see. Yeah, I take it off when I wash my head." Then wait as if thinking till they said, "Well, don't you take it off any other time?" And he'd say, "Oh yes, every Sunday I do when I go to church."

It was eleven years ago last March, Roland had his serious hat trouble, the time he was pouring cement for the subdivision going in along the Fakahatchee Strand over by the west coast and he went into this restaurant in Naples to have his dinner. At that time he was wearing a white Stetson that was seasoned and shaped the way rodeo contestants were wearing theirs, curved high on the sides but sort of snapped down in front. Some college boys in the place, drinking beer, would look over at him eating dinner with his hat on. He knew they were making remarks, snickering and laughing, bunch of dinks wearing athletic department sweat shirts and numbered jerseys. On their way out, number 79 stopped by Roland's table, stood there with his powerful shoulders and arms, hands on his hips, and said, "You always wear your hat when you eat?" The others, behind him, snickering some more. Roland said to 79, not looking up from his dinner, "Get the fuck away from me, boy, 'fore you end up in the salad." Number 79 reached for Roland's hat, got a fork stuck in his forearm and was letting out a howl when Roland belted him across the salad bar, smashing the sanitary see-thru top and sending the boy to the hospital for stitches, nearly as many as the number on his breakaway football jersey. Roland pleaded guilty to aggravated assault, was placed on a year's probation and paid hospital costs out of his pocket, $387, when they told him his Blue Cross wouldn't cover it.

He was in that same Lee County Circuit Courtroom a year later and this time they got him good. They told him to take off his hat and charged him with second degree murder: brought in witnesses who testified Roland had threatened to harm a land developer by the name of Goldman, who Roland had said owed him money; had been seen arguing with Goldman, provoking a fight, which was stopped; seen driving out toward Fakahatchee with Goldman, in his pickup truck, the day before he was found in a drainage canal, shot to death. No probation this time. Roland got 10 to 25 in Raford and served seven long years. Time to learn how to use his head and make valuable connections. Then he got out and never went back to the swamp again, outside of one time when a hotel owner fell behind on his vig and Roland drove out to the site of the Everglades jetport that was never completed, shot him and dumped him in a borrow pit a couple of alligators were nesting in. When Roland was called in for that kind of work now, he'd borrow Lionel Oliva's quick little eighteen-foot cruiser and head out toward the Stream, throw the guy over the side and take pot-shots at him till he disappeared.

Ed Grossi was a different situation.

Sometimes, when Vivian would continue to insist, making her point over and over, Ed Grossi would think, Yes, yes, yes. Talk, talk, talk. She was intelligent, but she was still a woman. She had insisted on driving him to Boca Raton; so he allowed her to, giving her that much, but not saying anything to her most of the way up Interstate 95.

Vivian said, "Why are you mad?"

He said, "I'm not mad."

She said, "I know when you're mad, whether you admit it or not."

He said, "If you know I'm mad, even when I'm not, then you should know what I'm not mad at." And thought, Jesus Christ, two grown people.

Grossi was mad—no, more irritated—because Vivian had said he was getting old. ("What restaurant was it?" "He didn't say." And because he hadn't asked Roland the name of the restaurant she had said, "You're getting old." Then had said she was sorry, but still wanted to know the name of the restaurant.)

He said now, "Let's forget it." Which meant they were finished talking about whether he was mad or not; though he could continue to feel irritated.

Give a woman a little, she'd try to become the boss. You had to keep her in line. As they turned into the Oceana, going down to the parking area beneath the condominium, Grossi said, "Let me off by the elevator and wait for me."

"I want to go with you," Vivian said.

"I said let me off by the elevator and wait."

Sit. Fetch. Sometimes you had to treat them like that.

"Maybe she needs a woman to be with her," Vivian said.

Grossi got out of the Cadillac and slammed the door. He had to wait for the goddamn elevator, feeling Vivian watching him. Then he was inside, the door closed, there, and he was in control again. He'd have a talk with Vivian, tell her a few simple rules. Like when a certain point is reached, keep your mouth shut, the discussion's over. Clara gave him no trouble, but he had to listen to her talk about her garden. Karen talked about her freedom. Karen—he'd give her anything she wanted and get that settled, not have to worry about her anymore. Ridiculous, having to stop and deal with women.

Grossi knocked and Roland opened the door almost immediately, Roland holding a decorative pillow.

"I was sleeping," Roland said.

Grossi came into the living room. "Where is she?"

"She's in the bathroom. Sounds like she's a little sick."

"She sleep at all?"

"Little bit. She won't talk to me no more."

Grossi moved down the hall to the bathroom. The door was closed. He knocked and said, "Karen?" There was no response, no sound from inside. Roland was coming along the hall now, still holding the small pillow. "You sure she's in here?"

"She might've passed out again," Roland said. "Better look in there and see."

Grossi turned the knob, expecting it to be locked. He opened the door carefully, not wanting to startle Karen or surprise her sitting on the toilet.

"Karen?"

He saw himself in the bathroom mirror. He looked toward the empty walkup tub. He looked back at the mirror and saw himself and Roland behind him. He saw Roland looking at him in the mirror, not quite grinning, but with an alert, knowing expression.

In his mind, in that moment, Grossi heard Vivian saying, "You're getting old," and his own voice saying, "Oh my God," and heard the heavy muffled gunshot hard against him, jabbing him, and saw in the mirror blood coming out of his shirtfront and on the mirror itself, his blood sprayed there as from a nozzle, seeing it in the same moment the sunburst pattern of lines exploded on the glass, his image there, his image gone.

Roland picked Grossi up, surprised how light he was, and dropped him in the deep bathtub.

He hadn't thought about the mirror breaking. He'd clean up the glass and the blood. Replace the mirror some other time, tomorrow maybe.

Right now he'd move Ed's car for the time being. Put it in a lot away from here, lock it up and walk back.

Wait till real late. Then the tricky part. Drop Ed out the window to land him in the sand. Better than taking him down the elevator in a box.

Drive him down to Miami International and put him in the trunk of Arnold's Jag, Florida ARN-268, parked in the Delta area.

Don't forget. Put the Smith in there too, grip and trigger wiped clean of prints, but with Arnie's partials all over the barrel.

Then drive Grossi's car to Hallandale, park it near Arnie's apartment.

Lot of work.

In the morning call the Miami Police. Change his voice to talk like a queer, one of Arnie's ex-buddies: Hi there. You don't know who this is, but I'll tell you where you boys can find a dead body. (Probably have to argue.) Just listen, asshole, or I'm gonna hang up and not tell you who done it or where you can locate him up in De-troit.

Work on that before morning.

What else?

Roland thought of something and he said, out loud, "Oh my. Oh my aching ass."

Something he had not thought of before and didn't know why he hadn't; but there it was, Jesus, the possibility.

What if Vivian had come here with Ed?

Vivian said, The son of a bitch. She backed the Cadillac up the parking aisle all the way past the street ramp, ready to turn and drive out.

But waited there and let herself calm down. What would it prove? Like stamping her foot or breaking dishes. Nothing. You won't change him, she thought. He's sixty-three years old, and he's the way he is. She put the Cadillac in "Drive" and, without accelerating, the car rolled down the aisle to the elevator door in the cement-block wall.

He would come down with Mrs. DiCilia and they would be busy attending to the woman, getting her home or someplace. And he won't even know you're angry at him, Vivian thought. The son of a bitch. He can ride up here all the way from North Miami without saying a word. But now when it was her turn to be mad, the son of a bitch wouldn't even know it.

Vivian again backed up the car to the street ramp. Go get something. Let him be waiting when she got back, Oh, have you been waiting long? I had to get some gas, since you don't keep any in your car.

The gauge indicated half full. But he wouldn't know that. Or go get a cup of coffee instead of waiting here like a chauffeur. Say to him, When do I get my hat and uniform?

Looking down the aisle, perhaps sixty or seventy feet, she saw the cowboy hat come out of the elevator.

She said, Oh God—

She hesitated. Ed could have sent Roland down to get her.

Roland was looking around, looking this way now. Staring, not sure if it was the right car. Then waving—Come on!—taking several steps into the aisle.

Vivian started up, with the Cadillac in reverse, and had to mash her foot on the brake to stop it—Roland coming toward her now—and had to look down at the automatic shift lever to get it into "Drive"—Roland running now, not waving Come on, what're you doing, but pumping his arms—as she pressed the accelerator, the car instantly leaping forward, and she had to turn hard to aim the front end up the ramp, scraping the concrete wall and hearing the tires shrieking and Roland's voice yelling something.

If she was wrong she would tell Ed later, I was wrong.

But she knew she wasn't wrong. She didn't know how she knew it but she did—going back in her mind, knowing she hadn't given Roland her telephone number. But at this moment having no idea where she could go to be safe.

16.

Karen read about it and saw film stories on television.

Ed Grossi's murder featured as a gangland/drug-related killing. His body found in the trunk of a suspected drug dealer's car at Miami International. The suspected drug dealer, Arnold Rapp, had fled; but soon after was apprehended in Detroit by fast-moving FBI agents and handed over to the Miami Police. Arnold Rapp had been charged with first degree murder—bond set at five hundred thousand dollars—and was being held awaiting trial in Dade Circuit Court, Criminal Division.

Karen ran, instinctively.

She went to Los Angeles to stay with her daughter, Julie. She told Julie about Ed Grossi, about the arrangement, about Roland. Julie seemed to listen. But they would talk and then Julie would run to the studio where she was doing voice loops for an Italian-made film or she would take milk shakes to Cedars-Sinai, to her husband Brian, who'd broken his jaw doing a stunt in a car-chase sequence.

At night Karen would sit in the living room of the house off Mulholland Drive and look down at the lights of Los Angeles.

Julie said, "I don't know, I guess I don't see the problem."

Karen said, "Then I must've left something out. If Ed Grossi is dead, then he can't change the arrangement, the trust fund. It goes on and on the same way, and I have to stay there the rest of my life."

"Well, get somebody else to change it."

"I'm afraid," Karen said, "I have a feeling, it's going to be in Roland's hands."

"Yeah? Well, then get Roland to change it. God, it sounds like something out here, dealing with these fucking producers, trying to find out who's in charge."

"He won't want to change it," Karen said. "If he does, he knows I'll leave in a minute."

"Well, if you like it there—" Julie said. "It's a good address, isn't it?"

"You mean—what? Is it fashionable?"

"Like here," Julie said. "We're in L.A., right? But you don't just say you're in L.A. Christ, L.*A.?* You say you live in the Hills. Or you get it across you're in 90046."

"I thought this was Hollywood," Karen said.

"God, no. There isn't any Hollywood, really. Or maybe 90069, down around where all the agents are, it's called Hollywood, but it's really Los Angeles County. See, if you're in Bel Air or Beverly Hills, like 90212, you don't even have to know your zip. But L.A.—Brian wanted to move to North Hollywood? I said, 'Brian, 91604 is *okay,* but it's not 90046 by any stretch of the imagination. It's living in the Valley, Brian. They say where do you live, you tell them Studio City, Sherman Oaks, some fucking place like that, they think you're in wardrobe or an assistant film editor."

Try again. Karen said, "I like my house, yes. But do I want someone forcing me to stay there?"

"Are you asking?"

Was she? Karen said, "I told you a little about Roland. I haven't told you everything, or what I'm afraid he's going to do."

"Well, at least you can talk to him," Julie said. "The director on this great epic spaghetti picture not only barely speaks English, he hasn't the slightest fucking idea what he's doing. He's got this translation for the dubbed version, it's written by an Italian, he's got me saying things like, 'I hated him. I think it is swell that he was slain.' Honest to God. I mean if you can talk to him, what's your problem, really?"

For five days Karen phoned Vivian Arzola at the Dorado Management office. Each day she was told Vivian was not in and each time the girl on the phone refused, politely, to give her Vivian's home phone number. On the fifth day Karen watched a brief television coverage of Ed Grossi's funeral on national news. She saw Roland, in his blue suit, serving as one of the pallbearers, but didn't recognize him immediately without his hat. There was no sign of Vivian in the film clip of activity outside St. Mary's Cathedral.

Later in the evening of the fifth day Maguire called. He said he had stopped by her house every day and finally Marta had given him the number in Los Angeles.

"In the Hills," Karen said. "Nine-oh-oh-four-six."

"What?"

"Do me a favor, will you? Tell Marta to save the Miami papers. But don't call her."

"You think I'd do that? Listen, how come you haven't called me?"

"I didn't have your number. But that reminds me," Karen said, "do you know how to find phone numbers?"

"You look in the book."

"Unlisted ones. I need Vivian Arzola's number. Or maybe you could find out where she lives." Karen spelled the name for him. "She works for Dorado Management but hasn't been there all week. It's very important. Okay?"

"Vivian Arzola," Maguire said.

She asked then, "Have you seen Roland?"

"Only on TV."

"Yes, I saw it too."

"When're you coming home?"

"Tomorrow," Karen said. There was a pause. "Do you miss me?"

She sat by herself in first class, no one in the seat

next to her; wore sunglasses much of the time; sipped three martinis and California red with her roast fillet; was polite to the flight attendants though she side-stepped conversation; read a book, *The Kefauver Story,* by Jack Anderson and Fred Blumenthal, which she had found in Frank's office, and reread a Xeroxed copy of an article from the June, 1951 issue of *American Mercury,* entitled "Virginia Hill's Success Secrets," she had got from the Fort Lauderdale Public Library. She thought of Cal Maguire. Don't tell him obvious things: like not to call the house or how to do his job. Be nicer. She thought of Roland Crowe and thought of Julie's line in the Italian film, changing the tense and applying it to Roland so that it came out, "I hate him. I think it would be swell if he were slain."

17.

The question in Maguire's mind, coming up more frequently now: What was he getting out of this?

He would recall and hear again the sound of Karen's voice on the phone. Almost impersonal. Nothing about being glad he'd called. Then asking if he missed her. Not saying she missed *him*. He had said, "You bet I miss you, a lot." He should have said, "Well, I think I do, but I'm not sure."

Friday, the day she was coming home—his day off—he drove to the DiCilia house again, left the Mercedes over by the garage doors, next to Marta's car, and rang the bell at the kitchen entrance.

Marta seemed surprised. "She isn't home yet."

"I came to see you," Maguire said. "You got any coffee on?"

In the kitchen that was like a restaurant kitchen, pans hanging from a rack above the table, he had to ask Marta to sit down. He could see she was aware of being alone with him in the house. "You know I'm her friend," he said. "You know I want to help her."

"Yes," Marta said.

"And you want to help her, too."

"Yes, but she said not to give anyone the number where she was."

"No, that was fine. I talked to her, and she's glad you did. She just forgot to mention it was okay to tell me." Forgot to mention—Christ. "She's got a lot on her mind"—looking for a way to get to the point—"but you know she's very grateful you told her about the tape recorder and all."

"I had to," Marta said. "It bothered me so much."

"Has Roland been back since she's gone?"

"Two days ago he came. He asked me where did she go. I told him I didn't know."

"Yeah? What'd he say to that?"

"He walked all over the house like he owned it, looking around in places he shouldn't."

"He take anything?"

"No, I don't think so."

"But you're not sure," Maguire said.

"He might have, yes. But I don't know."

"You told him you didn't know where Mrs. DiCilia was. Then what'd he say?"

"He threatened to do something to me." Marta hesitated. "So I told him, California."

"That was okay," Maguire said. "He's been listening to phone calls, he could've figured it out that's where she'd go. That's okay." He sipped his coffee and sat back, showing Marta he was at ease, not worried about it. "What I'd like to do, if I could, is talk to your brother."

"My brother?"

"From what I understand— See, she told me everything you told her. How he's quit, doesn't work for them anymore, all that. But I was wondering, maybe he could tell me a few things about Roland, the people he works for. Like Vivian Arzola. You know Vivian?"

Marta shook her head. "No, only the name."

"Or maybe your brother could tell me something about Roland that might help us. You never know."

"I could talk to him," Marta said.

"Could you call him? See if he'll meet me somewhere?"

"I think he may have gone to Cuba. Or he's going, I don't know."

"So maybe we don't have much time. You want to call him now? No, you can't do that, call from here." Maguire waited, letting Marta come up with the idea.

"I could go somewhere and call him. The drugstore by the causeway."

"Hey, would you do that?"

"Only the man's coming to fix the bed. He was suppose to come yesterday."

"Nuts." Maguire waited, thoughtful. When he'd given it enough thought, he said, "Why don't I stay in case the guy comes?" He paused, beginning to grin. "I know where the bed is."

Karen had walked from the patio into the house that night, was gone only a few minutes, and returned with a gun wrapped in tissue paper and forty-five new one hundred dollar bills.

He assumed she had put the gun back, somewhere in the bedroom— (He had thought of it lying with her in the broken-down bed. In one of the nightstands? In the dresser? Or behind the wall of mirrors in the closet?)

And assuming there were more new one hundred dollar bills hidden somewhere— (Lying in the bed he had thought of the money, too; first beginning to wonder what he was getting out of this.)

Maguire stood in the bedroom, alone in the house, Marta gone to phone her brother.

He had not told himself he was going to take the money; because at this point he could say, What money? You don't even know it's here. No decision to steal had been made. What he was doing—he told himself—was taking advantage of an opportunity. Seeing where he stood. Surveying the situation. So that if, in the end, he did have to grab something and run as an act of survival, for traveling expenses, it would be something portable and not the Louis XVI bergère or the Peachblow vases he'd have to wrap in newspapers and pack in a crate.

Where would she keep a lot of money?

In a safe.

But there was no safe in the bedroom or in the closet.

In the top dresser drawer he found a box of jewelry, unlocked, with some fine-looking pieces he assumed were real; though he'd never made a study of jewelry.

Next to the jewel box was the Beretta, still wrapped in tissue paper, loaded, a cartridge in the chamber. He rewrapped the gun, put it back in the drawer and told himself, okay, he knew where it was if he needed it, if he ever had to come running upstairs looking for a weapon.

But he was thinking mostly of 45 one hundred dollar bills, Series 1975, with consecutive serial numbers. Clean money, he assumed: thirty of the bills accepted at the post office without question when he'd bought the money orders. New but almost five years old, dating back to . . . Frank DiCilia. And thought of stories of how the wise guys always kept a lot of cash hidden away but handy, a stake, in case they ever had to run, their idea of traveling money. Sure, there had been a guy in Detroit, the feds had gone in with a search warrent, looking for something else, and found a couple hundred grand in the basement, hidden under the guy's workbench. Andre Patterson had said, Hey, 'magine hitting a man's house finding something like that? Pick out one of those old Eyetalian guys supposed to be retired. Andre couldn't even talk Cochise into it.

But the man dead, and happening to come across his stake, that was something else.

Except it could be anywhere in the house. Assuming it was here.

Maguire tried the door leading into the next room. Locked. He went into the hall and tried the outside door to the room. Locked. And thought, What's going on? Jewelry in an unlocked bedroom; the next room, the mystery room, locked. He remembered something, went back into the bedroom to the dresser, poked around in the top drawer again and found a half dozen keys, most of them to suitcases, one for a door lock.

He tried it, felt it slide in and turn, and stepped into

what had been Frank DiCilia's office at home. He saw the desk, the typewriter, the file cabinet—

He saw the photographs on the wall.

Photos of Karen. Enlarged photos or photostats, blowups of snapshots taped to the wall, blowups of newspaper photos in bold black and white.

He wasn't sure if they were all of Karen and then saw, that yes, there were shots of Karen alone, when she was much younger and not as good-looking as she was now, but with the same serious, secretive look. Karen in hats, Karen in dark glasses. Karen in summer dresses, bathing suits, wide-brimmed hats and dark glasses. Like a much younger Karen playing dress-up. There was one of a heavier Karen, which he realized, after a moment, wasn't Karen. It was someone else. A woman in a black wide-brimmed hat and dark glasses, black dress, and a fur stole. Dark glasses, though the picture had been taken inside, he was sure. There were several other shots of the woman he had not noticed before, mixed in with Karen's photos, blownup grainy photos like the one of Karen in the sunhat and bikini taken on the seawall. Karen's photos and those of the other woman were mixed together on the wall so that when he looked at the entire display he could believe they were all of the same person. Karen.

What was going on?

Maguire turned to the file cabinet. The key was lying on top. Then he looked at the wall of photos again.

If you did something like that, he thought, put up about a dozen pictures of yourself and a few of somebody who didn't look like you but did in a way, the expression, the dark glasses—trying for a certain look maybe? Going back to earlier pictures and finding the look there? An attitude? Why would you do it?

He opened the file cabinet—it was unlocked—began fingering through folders, papers. He came to a manila envelope, a big one, tightly packed, opened the fasteners, looked in and said, out loud, "My oh my." He took the envelope to the desk that was covered with newspaper pages, clippings, negative photostats—Karen in reverse; but didn't stop to look at them. Six packets of new one-hundred-dollar bills slid from the envelope. Five thousand dollars in each of five packets, five hundred in the sixth one. Tweny-five thousand five hundred dollars, 1975 Series bills, the same as the ones Karen had given him—right out of the sixth packet.

He thought of something. That the room had been locked because of the photos, not the money. He was sure of it.

He thought of something else. It was decision time. There it was, twenty-five grand, the most money he had ever seen at one time. Take it and run.

Or leave it.

Or lock it in the trunk of the Mercedes, which wouldn't be taking it because it was her car. The rationale: protecting it from Roland. But having it ready to grab.

Shit, if he was going to take it, take it.

He heard a sound, somewhere downstairs, a door slamming.

Marta came out from the kitchen to see Maguire in the front hall, at the foot of the stairs.

"I found him. My brother says okay. He'll meet you at Centro Vasco on Southwest Eighth Street. You know where it is? Maybe about Twenty-second Avenue, in Miami."

"I'll find it."

"But he doesn't see how he can help you."

"I've been trying to remember where I saw you before."

"At the fish place."

"No, I mean before that. Ten years ago," Maguire said.

He thought about it, looking past Jesus Diaz to the tables of people talking, having lunch at Centro Vasco, almost all of them Cuban.

"I know. The Convention Center, over on the Beach."

"Sure, I was there plenty times. I used to work out at the Fifth Street gym."

"You fought a guy by the name of Tommy Laglesia. He was doing something, I forgot what; everybody could see it but the ref."

"Butting me, the son of a bitch kept butting me in the face, the fucking ref don't say a word." Jesus straightened and leaned on his arms over the table. "You saw that, uh?"

"Yeah, it's funny—I used to go to fights, but not so much anymore."

"No, well, who's there to see?" Jesus said. "You saw that, uh?" He drank some of his beer, settling back again. "You know the other day—I didn't want to do nothing to you."

"No, I know you didn't," Maguire said. "But the other guy—I had to try and hit first, you know, try and get an advantage."

"Man, you hit him all right. He had to get stitches."

"I wish it'd been what's his name, Roland."

"Yeah, I wish it, too."

"Had enough of him, uh?"

"Man, forever."

"Have you seen him?"

"Last week. Then I see him on TV, but that's all. I don't work for him no more."

"Who else does?"

"Nobody. He's by himself."

"I was wondering," Maguire said, "with Grossi dead, what do you think might happen?"

"What do you mean, what might happen? To who?"

"Mrs. DiCilia if Roland, you know, is gonna still bother her."

"I don't know. He don't work for Mr. Grossi no more. Why would he?"

"Well, he sees a rich lady, all alone—"

"She got friends of her husband there. Mr. Grossi wasn't the only one."

"Yeah, maybe Vivian Arzola. You know where she is?"

"No, I don't know. She got a place in town; another place, I hear about in Keystone, but I don't know where."

"You know her phone number?"

"No, I don't know it."

"Mrs. DiCilia's anxious to talk to her." Maguire paused. "She have family in Miami?"

"No. Wait, let me think," Jesus said. "Yeah, I took something to her mother once for Vivian. She lives in Homestead. Vivian gives her, you know, the support."

"What kind of car does she drive?"

"Vivian? A white one with like a flower or something on the antenna. Some foreign car."

"You want to help Mrs. DiCilia find her?"

"I think I'm going to Cuba."

"If you don't go, I mean. She'll pay you whatever you think it's worth."

"Maybe I could do it," Jesus said.

"Sure, Cuba'll be there. You know where Roland lives?"

"Miami Shores. A place on Ninety-first Street called the Bayview."

"He live there alone?"

"Man, you think anybody would stay with him?"

"You want to go see him with me?"

"I don't think so. Not even stoned."

"How about with a gun?"

Jesus' hand was on his glass of beer. Looking at Maguire he seemed to forget about it.

"You ever do things like that?"

"If I have to."

"Yeah? Is that right?" Jesus continued to study Maguire. "Mrs. DiCilia, she want it?"

"She wants it, but she doesn't know she wants it, if you understand what I mean."

"She don't want to think about it."

"Something like that. But she'll pay you to be on her side, whatever you think it's worth," Maguire said. "Like five thousand, around in there? It's up to you."

"Around in there, uh? Let me think about it," Jesus Diaz said.

18.

After Ed Grossi's funeral, relatives and close friends came to Grossi's house on Hurricane Drive, Key Biscayne, to give Clara their sympathy and help themselves to a buffet. The friends and relatives who had not been there before, and even many who had, took time to walk up the street to 500 Bay Lane to see where Ed Grossi's neighbor, Richard Nixon, had lived. They came back saying shit, Ed's place was bigger.

Roland didn't care anything about historical sites. He got a plate of fettucini with clam sauce, a big glass of red and some rolls, and went over to sit with Jimmy Capotorto in the Florida room that was full of plants hanging all over, like a greenhouse.

Roland said, "It's a bitch, huh, something like this? Man, you never know."

Jimmy Cap had finished eating. He was smoking a cigar, looking out at the Bay, five miles across to South Miami. He asked Roland if the cops had talked to him.

Which was what Roland wanted to get over with. He said, "You kidding? Man, I'm the first one on their list. That Coral Gables Discount deal—shit, they picked me up before they even thought of you." Reminding Jimmy Cap, just in case.

Jimmy Cap said, "They tell me, say it was a setup, you know that. I say how do I know that? They say, this Arnold Rapp, he shoots Grossi and puts him in his own fucking car, come on, and leaves it at the airport? I say I only know what I read in the *Herald*."

"They give me the same shit," Roland said, "I didn't say it to them but I'll tell you, which you probably know anyway from Ed. This Arnie was a pure-D queer. I mean you look at him cross he'd piss his pants. I'd go over there to collect, have to shake him a little sometimes? He'd bust out crying. I'd say, Jesus Christ, you dink, cut your crying and pay up, that's all you got to do. See, he was a nervous little fella 'sides being a queer. It doesn't surprise me at all he fucked up, left Ed in his car. By then all he was thinking to do was run."

"Who fingered him?"

"I don't know for sure, but I believe it was a dink name of Barry used to work for Arnie. He got hurt and maybe he was pissed off, believed Arnie should've been the one hurt. See, it's hard to figure how these queers think."

"Don't do business with college boys," Jimmy Cap said.

"Hey, I told Ed that, the exact same words. Little fuckers, life gets hard, they go to pieces."

"Well, I'm not gonna worry about it," Jimmy Cap said. "What else you got?"

Here we go, Roland thought.

"Nothing important. Well, that DiCilia arrangement, you want to count that."

"Jesus, I don't want to even hear about it," Jimmy Cap said. "You handle it. Pay her off, forget about it. I don't give a shit where she lives."

"Let me look into it," Roland said. He dug into his fettucini, waiting to see if Jimmy Cap had anything else to say. No, it didn't look like it. Roland then said, "Vivian's been acting funny lately. You notice?"

"I didn't see her at the funeral," Jimmy Cap said.

"You haven't seen her around?"

"I don't know. I don't think so."

"She's in mourning or hiding or something," Roland said. "Nobody's seen her in a few days. She hasn't called or anything?"

"What would she call me for?"

"I just wondered. I don't know what's wrong with her. She's been starting to act strange."

"Fuckin' Cubans," Jimmy Cap said, "who knows? They're all crazy."

"I was thinking," Roland said, "she's liable to start bitching about this DiCilia arrangement. I mean when she finds out I'm handling it."

"Fire her," Jimmy Cap said. "I never could figure out what Ed saw in that broad anyway."

"Well, I'll see," Roland said. "I guess if I have to, I'll get rid of her."

Marta could not see Roland's face through the stained glass window in the door, but she could see his hat. She didn't want to open the door. But if she didn't, he could go around to the patio side, break something to get in. She didn't want to tell him Mrs. DiCilia had come home today and was in her room unpacking. But he would find out himself if he wanted. There was no way to stop him. It was too early to be picking up the tape: four o'clock in the afternoon. Marta opened the door, trying to be composed.

Roland was grinning at her.

He said, "You know, standing here I was thinking about another Cuban lady I liked to visit. She lives out the Tamiami on Beaver Road? I used to say to her, 'Honey, I just see your street sign I get a boner.' How you doing, Marty?"

"Mrs. DiCilia is very busy."

"Oh, she home? Well, we won't bother her," Roland said, coming in. "I just as soon fool around with you anyway."

"I have to go to the kitchen."

"Why don't we go your room instead?"

Both were down the back hall. Marta started that way and turned and didn't know where to go, Roland on her then, taking her from behind and pulling her in, Roland pausing to look up the stairway.

Marta said, "Please," and Roland said, "Mmmmm, you feel good," heavy workman's hands moving over the front of her white uniform, over her breasts, Roland saying, "We got a bra-zeer on under there? No, hey, we don't have no bra-zeer on, do we? Like our little titties free." The hands like old tree roots rubbing the white material, working down to her belly and thighs. "Let's see if we got any panties on." Grinning then, seeing Gretchen the schnauzer skidding across the hall floor at him. "Hey, Gretchie, hey Gretchie, how you girl? How's my girl, huh? You want some of this, Gretchie? No, you don't. This ain't for little doggies, this here is for—shit, where you going? Get her Gretchie!"

Roland reached down to take some playful swipes at the schnauzer, getting her to growl in fun, then went after Marta, hoping she was heading for the living room where he'd nail her on that big white sofa. But she ducked into the sitting room full of antiques and was almost to the French doors when he grabbed the hem of her white uniform from behind, yanked it up and heard it rip. Marta bounced off him and Roland fell hard against a wall of shelves, flung out an arm and destroyed several thousand dollars worth of Toby jugs and English china. Blueplate specials to Roland. He swiped at a Ralph Stevenson soup tureen ("View of the Deaf and Dumb Asylum") and there went another three grand . . . and Marta, half out of the uniform now, going through the French doors.

Karen heard the sound, glass shattering. She thought of a window, the French doors. She thought of Roland. Then heard another shattering of glass. Or china. From the sitting room. Voices, the sound coming faintly from outside. She heard the scream and knew it was Marta. Karen turned from the wall of photographs and saw them outside, below the window. Marta running, Marta in white panties, nothing else, running across the patio and past the swimming pool. Roland following after her, waving something white, Roland calling out, the words not clear. Karen raised the window. "I'm gonna get you, yes, I am, sugar, gonna eat you up." Roland stopping as Marta stopped, out on the lawn, and came around warily, holding her hands in front of her, beginning to circle back toward the house, facing Roland now, screaming again as he dug in and lunged toward her.

Karen turned from the window as if to run, to hurry. Then seemed to pause, almost imperceptibly, as she moved past the wall of photographs. She walked from the office into the bedroom, picked up the phone on the nightstand, dialed and said, "Operator, this is Karen Hill. I'm sorry, Karen DiCilia, 1 Isla Bahía. Would you call the police, please, and tell them to come right away? It's an emergency . . . Yes, Fort Lauderdale."

As soon as Roland heard the hi-lo sound of the police siren he walked away from the swimming pool and sank into a canvas patio chair. Marta remained in the pool, slightly stooped in about four feet of water. Both of them watched Karen come out of the house with the two police officers in dark brown uniforms and visored caps, both young looking and in condition, with serious-to-deadpan expressions. One of them took his sunglasses off and hooked them on his shirt pocket. No one spoke. Karen picked up a towel from the lounge chair, carried it to the broad steps at the shallow end of the pool and held it open for Marta. Roland and the police officers waited.

"Come on, it's all right," Karen said.

Roland and the police officers watched Marta step out of the pool and turn into the towel, pulling it around her.

"Tell them," Karen said.

The two police officers came onto the patio, looking at the two women, glancing at Roland.

Roland said, "How you doing?"

They didn't answer him. One of them said to Karen, "Is this the man?"

Karen nodded.

The police officer said to Roland, "Could I see your identification?"

Roland said, "Uh-unh. You got no reason to see it."

Both of the police officers turned to Roland with their deadpan expressions and stood without moving. The one who had spoken to him said, "Stand up and turn around."

Roland said, "Hey, cut the shit. You got a complaint? Let me hear what it is."

"Get up," the police officer said. "Right now."

The other one had his hand on his gun or his cuffs, Roland wasn't sure which. He looked over at Marta, shaking his head, then raised his hand. "Now come on. Since you didn't see nothing—before you start acting mean, who's your complaining witness?"

Karen said to Marta, "Tell them."

Marta looked from the police officers to Roland.

"Tell them," Karen said again.

"Somebody, I believe, got the wrong impression," Roland said. "It's all right, Marty, tell 'em. Heck, we were just playing around, weren't we?"

One of the police officers said to Marta, "Is this man a friend of yours?"

"I believe you could say we're a little thicker than that." Roland looked over at Karen and gave her a wink. "All of us here. We're old buddies. Me and Marty and Karen. Me and Marty's brother're very close. I see him all the time. Keep him out of trouble."

"He's threatening her," Karen said.

"Hey, Marty, am I threatening you?" Staring at her from beneath the low hat brim. "Go ahead, tell 'em."

"No, he's not," Marta said.

"Do you want to make a complaint against this man?" the police officer said.

"No," Marta said.

"Was he bothering you in any way?"

"No."

The police officer looked at Karen. Roland looked at her, too. She said, "Can I make a complaint?"

The police officer said to Marta, "How old are you?"

"Twenny-two."

"If this lady says there was an assault and it was

against you, then you'd have to file the complaint," the police officer said to Marta. "Are you afraid of this man? That he might hurt you?"

"No," Marta said.

"Or he might hurt somebody in your family?"

Marta shook her head. "No."

"You and him were just playing around?"

"Yes."

The police officer stared at her a little longer before turning to Karen. "If you want to make a complaint— Or maybe you ought to tell us what's going on here."

Karen said, "Do you really want to know?"

Roland liked that. He grinned, adjusting his hat, fooling with it. He said to Karen, "There you are. They want to hear the dirt." Roland's gaze moved to the police officers. He said to them, "You know who this lady is, Mrs. DiCilia? Was married to Frank DiCilia, good friend of Ed Grossi, recently passed away."

(Sure, they knew it. They'd have been sitting on Roland with a sap under his chin if it was some other backyard.)

"See, we have our disagreements, get into arguments like anybody else," Roland went on, as though he belonged here, part of the family. "But if we was to start ex*plain*ing everything to you, you'd be writing reports all night and on your day off . . . wouldn't you?"

Roland knew he had hit the nail on the head. The police officers stood there not saying anything. What did they see? A guy chases the maid into the swimming pool and the lady of the house gets pissed off. The lady hadn't yelled or had a fit. The lady was mad, yeah, but she seemed in control of the situation. ("Do you really want to know?") Pretty cool about it. It took the policemen off the hook and it made Roland happier'n a pig in shit. The lady saw clearly the position she was in. Call the police and then what? Call them every day?

Roland, in the front doorway, watched the white Lauderdale police car with it's red bubble, drive over the bridge to Harbor Beach Parkway. He'd pulled it off, made his point.

Roland said over his shoulder, "I knew you were up there watching. You enjoy the show?"

No answer from her.

The cops had eyed his Cadillac and right now were probably calling the Communications Center to punch the code on his license number. Those guys were going to shit when they got the report; but they wouldn't come back now without a heavy charge and backup.

Karen, standing behind him in the hall, said, "Are we going to talk?"

Roland turned, closing the door. He studied Karen, trying to make up his mind about something.

"You're different'n before. You know it? You're a lot calmer. I don't mean you're ever excitable, but there's something different about you. You got something bothering you you're holding in?"

"You talk a lot," Karen said, "but you never get to the point." She turned and went into the living room.

Roland followed her, looking up at the high-beamed ceiling, impressed with the size of the room every time he came in here.

"I believe I owe you a few bucks. I broke some plates."

Karen said, "Tell me what you want." She stood by the fireplace. She felt like moving but didn't want to pace in front of him.

Roland eased into a deep chair. His hat brim touched the cushion of the backrest and he hunched forward a little.

"What're you offering me?"

"How about twenty-five thousand?"

"Cash? In new hundred dollar bills?"

Karen stared at him.

Roland stared back. He said, "How come you got all those pictures upstairs?" He pulled his Ox Bow down closer to his eyes so he could rest his head against the chair.

"Did you take the money?"

"No, it's there. I figure it's for cigarettes and bird feed, uh?"

"I'm waiting for you to come out and say it," Karen said. "What you want."

"I'm not bragging or anything," Roland said, "but ladies have asked me that before. 'What do you want?' they say, 'anything.' "

"I haven't said 'anything.' "

"Not yet. See, the fact you got four million bucks, sort of—the proceeds of it—don't make you any different from the other ladies asked me what I wanted. And I was in no position to be as nice to them as I am to you. See, Ed Grossi passed on before he changed anything, and guess who they put in charge?"

"I don't believe you," Karen said.

"Call Jimmy Cap. Ain't nobody higher'n Jimmy."

Karen started to move from the fireplace. She caught herself, moving to be moving, made herself stand motionless, relax, and put her hand on the rough beam that served as a mantel. Why was it so easy for him? Roland. The way he'd handled the police; refused to stand up or answer them. The convenience, the timing of Ed Grossi's death. She wanted to probe, ask questions, insinuate—

And found she didn't have to. Roland said, "You don't know for sure Ed was gonna change anything, let you off, as you told me one time. No, I believe he meant to leave it as is. So you're lucky, aren't you, the way things turned out. Now you got somebody you can see eye to eye with."

"The way it happened to turn out," Karen said.

"Yeah, I don't mean we should go out and celebrate Ed's passing, but it does make it easier for all concerned."

"That he happened to die," Karen said, staying with it.

"Hey, they got the guy," Roland said. "Don't try and mix me up in that. No, all I'm saying, you work hard and sometimes you get lucky. And here we are, huh?"

"You had something to do with his death," Karen said.

"I know the boy did it, that's all. Ask the police, I already talked to them."

Karen wanted to say, And Vivian, who's also in this. Where's Vivian? But she held back, aware of herself standing at the mantel, alone with the man who wore his hat in the house, the backcountry gangster, the Miami Beach hotdog, the good-ol' boy with his boots on the coffee table—God—making herself remain calm while she felt the stir of excitement, and thought, as she had the first time he came here—you can handle it.

Play it his way. You can take him.

Karen said, "You still haven't said anything, have you? What you want."

"Yeah, I said ladies have offered me things, wanting to be nice."

"How much is nice?"

"No, it's got to be what you *want* to give. You don't understand, do you?"

"I'm having a little trouble," Karen said.

"Look, you got four million bucks, the proceeds of it. You got everything you should want or need. But if you leave here you're cut off, the funds end."

"I'm aware of that."

"I'm reviewing the situation. I can't see you leaving and giving up four million bucks."

"I can't either," Karen said.

"But your fooling-around love-life is also curtailed, huh?"

"It looks like it."

"Unless you and me get something going."

"You mean all I have to do is go to bed with you?"

Roland grinned. "You mention it, I get horny. But see, I'm not going to force you. As I told you the first time I was here, I'm your boy cuz I'm the only one you got."

"I go to bed with you," Karen said. "Then what?"

"You *ask* me to go to bed."

"All right, I ask you. Then what happens after that?"

"We live happily ever after."

"You move in here?"

"Tomorrow, you want me to."

"It's not just money then. Even a whole lot."

"Money?" Roland said. "Shit, I want the money and everything that goes with it. You, the whole setup."

"But you're not going to use force, intimidation."

"Other than keeping your dink boyfriends away so's you become sex-starved."

"If it's simply between you and me," Karen said and paused. "You don't have a chance."

There was Roland's grin, showing he was enjoying himself and liked the situation. He said, "We might've got off on the wrong foot and all. But, listen, you're gonna find I'm really a sweet person."

19.

Maguire saw the Cadillac Coupe de Ville in the drive as he turned onto Isla Bahía. He continued past the house, seeing the dead-end ahead at the canal, and came to a stop.

Nowhere to hide. He knew it was Roland's car in the drive: the same one he had watched Roland get in when they came out of the Yankee Clipper, Maguire hanging back so Roland wouldn't see the Mercedes.

He'd see it now. Maybe looking at it out the window right this minute.

Well, he could turn around and get out of here, quick. Or he could go in the house— Didn't we meet someplace before? He didn't know how to play it. He didn't know how Roland would react. But Roland was there and what if right at this moment Karen needed help? Shit. Andre Patterson said he had nerve; but that was going into a place ready, knowing what you were going to do, having a good idea what the reaction would be. This was way different. Goddamn Roland—he didn't know anything about him except he was built like a six and a half foot tree stump and had the hands and the reach and a hide it would be hard to even dent, 'less you hit him with a tire iron. From behind.

He could feel them watching him. Roland and Karen. Shit. He backed up the car, all the way past the drive, and turned in.

Marta's hair was combed but looked wet, like she'd just washed it. Maguire said, "Anybody home?"

"He's here," Marta said.

"I know he is. Where are they?"

"I think you better not come in."

"It's all right," Maguire said. "I'm not gonna hurt him."

Both of them watched Maguire make his entrance, appear and wait to be invited into the living room. Karen by the fireplace, Roland seated in a deep chair with his hat on.

Gretchen came over, sniffed at Maguire's legs and went back to Roland who reached down, giving Gretchen his hand to play with, saying, "You smell the dead fish on him, Gretchie? Huh, do you? Pee-you but it stinks, don't it?"

Karen watched without moving, though she didn't seem tense; her eyes following Gretchen to Roland, then returning to Maguire with a mild expression, Maguire thinking, what if the dog was a test and he had flunked it? Maybe that's what dogs were for. Maybe that was the time, just now, to stoop down and play with Gretchen and try to think of doggie talk. He wondered how Karen was going to handle it, what she'd say—

But it was Roland who invited him in.

"Hey, come on'n sit down. You son of a gun, you knew it was me the other night in the bar, didn't you?" Roland grinned. "You tell her that story about the woman with the parrot?"

"I don't believe he has," Karen said, a little surprised.

Roland waved his arm. "Come on in here and sit down, partner."

Maguire walked around the couch facing the fireplace and eased into it at the end away from Roland. He looked at Karen: her eyes on him but not telling him anything; guarded, or only mildly curious. Then looking at Roland as he spoke.

"This woman had a sick parrot she kep' in the bathroom," Roland said. "Christ, spent weeks nursing it back to health, got it all well again and the parrot, you know what it did? Tried to get a drink of water in the toilet and drowned."

Karen said, "That's the story?"

"He didn't tell it right," Maguire said. "You don't say the parrot was trying to get a drink."

"What was it doing," Roland said, "taking a piss?"

"No, it's the way the woman told it," Maguire said. "The idea, like this is a moving experience, she's been waiting for somebody to come by so she can tell it. But then when she does, it's at the wrong time. You know what I mean?"

"Christ, I know them women better'n you do."

"I don't doubt that. I'm talking about this particular woman. All alone, nobody to talk to."

"Waiting for somebody to come give 'er a jump," Roland said. "I know exactly what you're talking about. But what do you believe that parrot was doing in the toilet?"

Karen looked from Roland to Maguire.

"I believe it wanted a drink of water," Maguire said, "but that isn't the point."

"If that's what the goddarn parrot wanted, then say it," Roland said. "Otherwise it don't make sense what the parrot was doing in the toilet."

"You tell it your way, I'll tell it mine," Maguire said.

Karen looked from Maguire to Roland.

"Shit yeah, I'll tell it my way," Roland said. "You leave out the best part. Or you could say—yeah, you could say the parrot *was* trying to take a piss and it drowned. That'd make it a better story."

"You miss the whole point," Maguire said.

"Miss the point—you dink, I *lived* out there with those people half my life."

"I believe it," Maguire said.

"What's that mean, that remark?"

"You say you lived out there, I believe it. That's all," Maguire said, looking at the redneck son of a bitch sitting there like it was his house, feet up, playing with the dog. Be cool, Maguire thought. Take it easy. But Karen was watching, and he had to say something else.

He said, "You always wear your hat in the house?"

"You want to say something about it?"

"I asked you a simple question, that's all."

"You want to take it off me?"

"No, I think it looks good on you. Tells what you are."

Black metal tongs and a poker hung at the end of the fireplace behind Karen.

"And what do you say I am?" Roland said.

"Let's see. You wear a range hat and cowboy boots," Maguire said, "and that suit"—aware of Karen listening—"I'd have to guess you're with a circus."

"You guessed it," Roland said, starting to pull himself out of the chair, ignoring Gretchen jumping at his leg. "And you know what I do at the circus?"

Karen could say something now. Right now would be a wonderful time for her to get into it. But Karen watched them without saying a word.

Maguire paused.

Three steps to the black iron poker—if he could get it off the hook in time.

He said, "Let's see. Are you one of the clowns?"

Roland said, "No, I'm not one of the clowns." Standing now, ten feet away. "I'm the Wildman of the Big Swamp, and what I do"—moving toward Maguire now—"I take smartass little dinks that smell of fish and I tear 'em asshole to windpipe and throw 'em away."

Karen said, "Why don't you sit down?" But much too late.

Maguire pushed off the sofa, going for the fireplace. Roland reached him easily, swiveled a hip, caught Maguire in a headlock against his side and held him there. Roland squeezed his hands together to apply pressure, and Maguire gagged, feeling his breath cut off.

"Leave him alone," Karen said, in a mild tone. Maguire hearing it and thinking, Christ, *tell* him! Make him! He couldn't move; he tried to push against Roland, tried to reach around to get a grip on the man's hips; but Roland squeezed, and Maguire felt himself grow faint.

"So this here's the porpoise man," Roland said. "Hey, partner, what do you do, play with them porpoises all day? They get you excited, watching 'em? Little shithead comes in here, starts flapping his mouth." Roland held Maguire with one arm around his neck and began to rub the knuckles of his free hand into Maguire's scalp. "Hey, shithead, how's that feel? Give you a knuckle massage. I'll give you a knuckle sandwich I ever see you around here again. How's that feel, huh? Kinda burn, does it?"

Karen said, "That's enough. Stop it."

Roland took hold of Maguire's right arm as he released him and bent the arm up behind Maguire's back, lifting him up, raising his face that was flushed and stung, trying not to yell out but, Christ, his shoulder was about to twist out of place.

"That way," Roland said. "Go on, toward the hall there."

Karen watched, still at the fireplace, remembering something like this from a long, long time ago: Karen Hill watching two seventh grade boys on the school playground. The headlock; the Dutch rub, they called it then; the arm bent behind the back—

"Go on, get your ass out of here." Roland in the hall now, giving Maguire a shove as he released him.

Maguire kept going to the front door. He saw Marta in the doorway that led to the back hall, watching him, sympathetic. Or maybe not. Maybe thinking, So much for him.

Roland called out, "Leave the car!"

Maguire was opening the door when he called again. "Wait a minute!"

Maguire waited, looking outside at the faint, early evening sunlight, not turning around. Roland came up to him.

"I want to ask you something," Roland said, his tone mild again. "You're over there with them porpoises all the time—you ever see 'em do it?"

"Do what?"

"You know, *do* it."

"Every night," Maguire said.

"No shit, every night, huh? Hey, you suppose I could come over sometime and watch?"

Jesus Diaz said to the woman in the doorway, her TV on loud behind her, "I know he be coming home soon. See, I know where he is. He told me to wait for him."

Aunt Leona said, "It's all right with me if you wait. Sit anywhere you want." Pointing to some old lawn chairs.

"I mean I'm supposed to wait inside his place." In case Roland followed Maguire for some reason, Jesus wasn't going to have Roland see him sitting here at the Casa Loma. He'd go to Cuba right now before he'd let it happen.

"Well, I don't know," Aunt Leona said.

"See, we old friends. I'm not going to steal nothing."

Man, all that to get in his apartment. If it was dark he would have walked in himself. As it turned out it became dark as he sat watching Maguire's black and white TV and drinking some of Maguire's rum. A good-looking girl in a red T-shirt came in. Jesus stood up and said he was waiting for his friend. The good-looking girl said, "Lots of luck," and went out. Finally, when Maguire walked in the door he looked surprised, though more drunk than surprised.

"I saw your two cars at the DiCilia house," Jesus Diaz said. "But you're all right, uh? You want to know who I saw before that?"

Maguire poured himself a rum over ice. "I don't know, do I?"

"I saw Vivian Arzola. I look around Keystone all day. Nothing. I drive to her mother's place in Homestead. There she is."

"That's nice," Maguire said. "Tell the lady. Hold your hand out like this, she'll give you a tip."

"Right away Vivian's scared to death when I see her. I say take it easy, I'm not going to hurt you. I jes want to tell you Mrs. DiCilia want to talk to you. She look at me like she don't trust me. Something is strange about her. You know? I leave, but I wait around in my car. Pretty soon she come out with a suitcase. I follow her little foreign car back to Miami to a house on Monegro. You know where I mean? In Coconut Grove, little pink house there. She goes in, a little while later I go up, ring the bell. No answer. Shit, I know she's in there. But what's the matter with her? You listening?" Jesus Diaz looked at Maguire stretched out on the bed now, holding his drink. "I ring the bell again. Nothing. So I open the door with these keys I have, you know? I look through the house. She's hiding in the bedroom, man, in the closet. She say, 'Oh, please don't kill me.' I say, 'What do I want to kill you for?' She say, 'I won't tell, I promise you.' I say, 'You won't tell what?' You listening? We talk some more, talk some more, I'm very nice to her, we talk about our mothers, I tell her I quit the business, I'm going to Cuba. She say, 'I want to go with you.' I say, 'Why?' We talk some more. You know what she's scared of? Of course, Roland. You know why she scared? Hey, you listening? Because she know Roland killed Ed Grossi."

"I'm listening," Maguire said.

20.

Lesley was saying into the mike, "That little hole there on top of Misty and Gippy's head is called their blowhole. It's just like your nose. If they get water in there they could catch pneumonia, pleurisy, or even drown. So please don't splash them. 'Sides if you do, they're gonna splash everybody back." Pause. "And no one has *ever* won a water fight with a dolphin."

Lesley, Karen decided—walking away from the Porpoise Play Pool—was cute but a little tacky. Probably not too bright, either.

She looked in at the grandstand show pool again, walked around to the refreshment stand and there he was. At a picnic table having coffee.

"Why aren't you working today?"

Maguire looked up. "I'm trying to get fired."

"I think I asked you once before, why don't you quit?"

"Pretty soon."

Karen said, "I'm sorry about yesterday."

"Yeah, I could see, the way you were standing there watching."

"What did you expect me to do, hit him?" Karen sat down at the picnic table. Maguire, stirring his coffee with a plastic stick, didn't look up. Karen watched him. "I just found out something you wouldn't tell me. 'These are Atlantic bottle-nosed dolphins. The porpoise is a much smaller animal, nervous and high strung, practically untrainable,' " Karen said, giving it a little of Lesley's southern Ohio accent. " 'But we call 'em porpoise so you won't get 'em mixed up with the dolphin *fish* you see on menus in some of Florida's finest restaurants. Don't worry though'—you all—'when you order it, you are not eating Flipper.' You think I could get a job here."

"Talk to Brad. Tell him you need the money."

"Are we a little pouty today? I thought you handled it pretty well, considering everything. At least you stood up to him."

"I did, huh?"

Karen picked up his coffee and sipped it. "Too much sugar." She put it down again. "I brought the car for you—if you can drive me back."

"What else can I do for you?"

Karen studied him, waiting for him to look at her. "Why're you taking it out on me? There wasn't anything I could do."

"I got the feeling you didn't much care," Maguire said, "one way or the other."

"Would it've helped if I'd screamed, kicked him in the shins?"

"It might've."

"The police were already there once, and did nothing."

"For what? You called them?" Maguire looked up, interested.

"Roland was making a point. That he could hit close to home and the police wouldn't do anything about it. He pretended he was going to rape Marta, and I got excited and called the cops."

"You got excited?" Maguire said.

"I was afraid he was going to hurt her. I didn't know it was an act."

"Then when you realized it," Maguire said, "you were Cool Karen again?"

"What're you trying to say?" She put on a little frown, but it didn't indicate much concern.

"You've got this guy hanging on you," Maguire said, "but you don't seem too worried anymore. Like, so what? What's the big deal? I don't know if you've given up or you don't care."

"Guess what he wants?" Karen said. "He finally said it. Everything, including me."

"See? That's what I'm talking about. You think it's funny or what?"

"He said I'll reach the point where I'll *want* to give him everything, because he'll be my only chance."

"You believe that?"

"Well—he's got more confidence than anyone I've ever met."

"He's got more bullshit, and that's what he's giving you. He's gonna look for the opening, set you up and take whatever he can. And if you're laying there with your head broken, that's tough shit."

"He likes me."

"He may, but that's got nothing to do with it."

"But you see, his self-confidence, that's the flaw," Karen said, leaning closer over the table. "What does he base it on? Not much. There's considerably less to Mr. Roland Crowe than he realizes. Watching you two yesterday—you know what it was like? Two little boys showing off in front of a girl. Arguing about the parrot—I couldn't believe it."

"You didn't get it."

"No, I assumed you were putting him on, but he was serious. I'd look at Roland. *This* is the one who's giving me trouble? I thought of something Ed Grossi told me once, about being concerned with people who turn out to be lightweights."

"Ed Grossi," Maguire said. "He told you that, huh? You want some more advice?"

"What?"

"Forget Ed Grossi's advice. Talk to Vivian Arzola."

Roland said to Lionel Oliva, "How can you live in this dump? Goddamn place ain't any bigger'n a horse trailer."

"We manage."

"Get her out of here."

Lionel turned to the woman cooking something for him on the tiny stove. She edged past them without looking at Roland and stepped out of the trailer. Roland bent down to watch her through the window—big Cuban ass sliding from side to side as she walked out of Tall Pines toward S.W. Eighth Street.

"You want the boat?" Lionel Oliva said. "Take somebody out?"

"Not just yet." Roland straightened up, making a face as he looked at Lionel. "You drink too much, you know it?"

"I like to drink sometime, sure."

"You like to live in this stink?"

"I don't smell nothin'."

"Jesus, look at the place. You work for me, you're gonna have to clean yourself up."

"I work for you now?"

"I want you to see if you can find Vivian Arzola. Her and you both used to pick oranges, didn't you?"

"Man, a long time ago."

"Well, go look up some of your old buddies still around. See if anybody's seen her lately."

"How come I work for you now," Lionel Oliva said, "you don't get Jesus?"

"He went to Cuba, you dink. You were sitting there when he told me."

"No, he never went to Cuba. I see him talking to a guy in Centro Vasco yesterday."

"You see him again, tell him to call me," Roland said. "Tell him I don't hear from him and run into him on the street, I'll bust his little bow legs and wrap 'em around his dink head."

Roland got out of that smelly house trailer. He'd look around some for Vivian; stop in and see Karen, make her day a little brighter. First, though, he was going to go home and pick up a firearm to carry on him or keep in the car. There was too much going on now not to be ready for what you might least expect.

Vivian Arzola said to Jesus, when he returned in the morning, "I have to think about it."

"Think about what? She wants to help you."

"How? All I do is endanger myself telling somebody else."

"Trust her," Jesus said.

"All right, but only Mrs. DiCilia. If she brings police, I don't know anything."

"Her and one other, a friend that's helping her. This is his idea, but I can't tell you anything else."

"You can't tell me, I'm supposed to tell him everything. All right, the two of them. And you," Vivian said. "Any more, I have to rent chairs. You see what they do to this place? Sneak out before the first of the month, leave all this crap. Look at the condition, the dirt. Five years I've owned this place, I've never made any money."

"What time?" Jesus said.

"Late, after it's dark. I don't know, nine o'clock. You drop them off—what kind of car?"

"I don't know yet."

"Forget the whole thing," Vivian said.

"Wait, let me think. Gray Mercedes-Benz."

"You drop them off. I don't want the car in front."

"What else?"

"Tell them I'm not going to the police. If that's what they want, they're wasting their time. No police in this. I see a policeman, I don't know anything you're talking about."

"If you say it. Anything else?"

"A gun," Vivian said.

"What kind?"

"What kind, one that shoots. I don't care what kind. A big one."

"Take it easy," Jesus said. "You got nothing to worry about."

21

Jesus, driving the Mercedes, dropped them off in front of the pink stucco house on Monegro Avenue within a minute or so of nine o'clock, telling them he would drive around and come back at exactly 9:30.

Maguire wondered if all this was necessary: like synchronizing their watches, everyone very grim, Karen wearing dark glasses—why? So who wouldn't recognize her?—but he didn't say anything. Or comment, make a harmless smart remark about Vivian letting them in with the lights off, taking them back to the kitchen and closing the door to the hall before turning on the kitchen light. Maguire was glad he'd kept quiet. Even seeing Vivian for the first time—not anything like the stylish woman Karen had described in the car—Maguire realized how frightened she was. Vivian looked like she had been on a drunk for several days; combed her hair maybe, but had forgotten about makeup. For the first few minutes they were in the kitchen, he had never seen anyone so tense. Maguire poured the coffee. He lighted three cigarettes for Vivian, while she told them about driving Ed Grossi to Boca Raton and seeing Roland and barely getting away from him.

"Why won't you go to the police?" Karen asked her.

Vivian said, "Because he'll kill me. Why do you think?"

"But he'll be in jail."

"He'll be out on bond, he won't be in jail."

"Well—the police will protect you."

"Excuse me," Vivian said, "but I worked for Ed Grossi twelve years. If they want a person dead, the person's dead. This is what Roland does, it's his job."

Karen said, "To kill people?"

Maguire watched her. She seemed more fascinated by the idea than startled or shocked.

Vivian said, "Yes, of course. He can go to prison and pay somebody else to do it. Or, if he wants to himself bad enough, he waits till he gets out. Don't you know that? They convict him, I have a nice time for ten years. Then what?"

"They've charged someone else with his murder," Karen said.

"Arnold Rapp, I know that," Vivian said. "It's too bad, but I'm not giving my life for Arnold Rapp."

"It's almost nine-thirty," Maguire said.

Karen, seated close to Vivian, looked up from the kitchen table. "Why don't you go with him? Come back at ten."

Why? What were they going to talk about? He couldn't see Karen's eyes behind the glasses. She sat in the dirty kitchen of the house on Monegro in the Cuban quarter working something out. As though she did this all the time.

Maguire went out to the curb and got in the Mercedes as it came to a stop.

"Where is she?"

"We come back in a half hour."

Jesus drove off. "I went up to Eighth Street. I saw a guy there he say Roland's looking for me. Shit. Man, I got to go to Cuba or do something."

Maguire didn't say anything, looking at the people sitting in front of their houses and the ones on the sidewalk watching the silver-gray Mercedes-Benz drive by.

"What do you think about Vivian?" Jesus said.

"I think she's scared."

"No, I mean do you think she'd pay us something? Why not, uh?"

They picked up Karen at 10. Maguire slid behind the wheel and Jesus got in back as far as S.W. Eighth, where they dropped him off. Maguire cut over to 95 and headed north to Lauderdale. Karen had taken off her glasses. She sat holding them, silent.

"Well?" Maguire said.

Karen didn't say anything.

"What else you find out?"

"Nothing, really."

"She still won't go to the police."

"The day Roland dies, she will. If the other man is still in prison. He kills people," Karen said.

"You mean Roland."

"Yeah. He kills people."

Maguire said, "Do you want me to stay with you tonight?"

Karen took a long time to answer. She said, "Not tonight, okay? I'd like to do some quiet thinking."

"That's the only kind," Maguire said, keeping it light, but feeling a little hook inside him. Something was going on.

They drove in silence; left the freeway and headed east toward the ocean through light evening traffic, across the 17th Street Causeway and past Seascape, Maguire's other world, dark. Maguire picturing the dolphins by themselves, surfacing in moonlight within their pools and tanks.

He said to Karen, "When I worked at the dolphin place down on Marathon, ten years ago—I didn't tell you, did I, I got arrested for willful destruction of property?"

Karen didn't say anything.

"You listening?"

"You were arrested for willful destruction of something."

"The fences," Maguire said. "They didn't have tanks down there, they had wire fences built out from the shore and the breakwater. Like pens they kept the dolphins in. Different pens that were attached to each other. One night I went out there with some tinsnips and cut the fences."

Karen said, "You freed the dolphins?"

"Yeah. They swam out to sea."

"That's remarkable." She kept looking at him now.

"Unh-unh, the remarkable thing," Maguire said, "as soon as they got hungry they all came back to the pens and never left again. . . . They didn't want to be saved. They just wanted to play games."

22.

Jesus Diaz was taking his suit and some pants to the dry cleaner, getting ready for his trip, whenever it was going to be. He was walking past the place on the corner of Eighth Street and Forty-second Avenue that gave spiritual readings and advice, when the car turned the corner, stopped hard, and the voice said, "Hey!"

Jesus almost dropped the clothes and took off. But it was Lionel Oliva motioning him to come over to the car.

"I thought you went to Cuba."

"Pretty soon."

"I got your job. Man, it's a lot of work."

"Keep it," Jesus said.

"What's he want with Vivian Arzola?" Lionel asked.

Jesus moved in closer, stuck his head in the window, resting his clothes against the dusty car.

"He's looking for her?"

"He came to the trailer yesterday, insulted me, then hired me to find her. What does the pimp give you for a job like this?"

"Different amounts. What he feels like," Jesus said. "You have any luck?"

"That's what it was," Lionel said. "You know she owns some houses to rent. I was talking to this guy used to know her, lives in the Grove. He said yeah, this house of Vivian's on Monegro was vacant for a month. But then he saw a light on, and he thinks he saw her go in there the other day. So I went over, I look in the window. There she is in the hall, going into the kitchen or someplace. I knock on the door, no answer."

"She probably don't want to see anybody," Jesus said.

"Stuck up, owning all those houses," Lionel said. "Fuck that, I'm not going to bother with her."

"I wouldn't," Jesus said.

"Let Roland see if he can talk to her."

"You tell him yet?"

"Yeah, I just called him a few minutes ago."

Ten-fifteen, another fifteen minutes before show time, Brad Allen was addressing his "gang"—Lesley, Robyn, Hooker, Chuck, and Maguire—sitting around on the lower grandstand benches, while Brad, in pure white, stood between them and the pool. The main-show dolphins would surface and watch them from the holding pens along the side. Brad half-turned to point across the pool to the deck that served as the stage.

"What we'll do, we'll light some paper in some kind of shallow metal container. Maguire, you'll still be backstage. Wait there after the intro. So you'll ring the firebell."

Seascape opened at ten. There were people on the grounds already looking around, coming past the roped-off grandstand area and looking in, wondering what all those kids in the red T-shirts were doing sitting there. No, they weren't all kids, were they?

Robyn said, "Brad, it's a dynamite idea, but do you light the paper and you're the one that yells fire?"

"No, you're right," Brad said. "*You* light the paper. That's good thinking, Rob. And I'll be distracting the audience, my back turned to you."

Maguire saw Jesus Diaz approach the chain across the entrance and the sign hanging from it that said: THIS AREA CLOSED UNTIL SHOWTIME, Jesus looking at the sign and then looking in anxiously at the group sitting in the grandstand. Maguire raised his arm. He stood up.

"Sit down," Brad said.

"I got to talk to that guy for a minute."

The others were turning to look up at Maguire and then over to the Cuban waiting by the chain.

"Sit down till we get this straightened out," Brad said. "I turn around, I see it and yell, 'Fire!' Cue for the firebell. No, wait'll I say, 'This is a job for Smokey the Dolphin.' Yeah. Then ring the bell. Then Hooker? You've got the hat on Dixie, right?"

"Right," Hooker said.

"Maguire, sit down."

"I just have to see the guy a minute."

"When we're through," Brad said. "Okay, Hooker—you give Dixie the signal."

"Right."

"She comes over, gives a couple of tail flaps—"

Maguire was staring at Jesus, trying to read his mind.

"—and puts out the fire."

"He knows where she is!" Jesus called out to him.

Maguire was moving.

"Where you going? . . . Maguire!"

Brad and the "gang" watched him hurdle the chain—brush the sign with his foot, causing it to jiggle—and take off with the Cuban.

"Any idea where he's going?" Brad asked.

"He probably don't know himself," Lesley said. "He's weird."

Virginia Hill was really Virginia Hauser, or Virginia Hill Hauser; but no one referred to her by that name. She was Virginia Hill, who told the Kefauver Crime Committee in 1951 that men kept giving her money because they were friends. Period. She didn't know exactly how much she had. Yes, she knew Bugsy Siegel, he was one of the friends. No, she didn't know what he did for a living.

Karen wore a white scarf over her hair (tied in back), sunglasses, and a beige and blue striped caftan that reached to the brick surface of the patio.

She said to the feature writer from *The Goldcoaster*, a pleasant, nice looking but unyielding girl by the name of Tina Noor, "I was Karen Hill much longer than I was Karen Stohler or Karen DiCilia, that's all I'm trying to say. I think of myself as Karen Hill." And only thinking about the other Hill, not mentioning her. "How do you think of yourself?"

"As Tina Noor."

"You're married."

"Yeah."

"But you don't think of yourself, ever, as who you used to be?"

"Yeah, but that's exactly the point. I'm not really that person anymore."

"Well, we're different," Karen said. "You want to sell magazines, and I want to maintain my identity. Karen Hill. Don't you think it sounds better?"

"It's a nice name," Tina Noor said, "but no one knows who Karen Hill is."

"I do."

"I mean everyone's familiar with Karen DiCilia. You were in the papers again when Ed Grossi was killed. People are interested in what you think about . . . what it's like to be associated with those people and live a normal life."

"A normal life," Karen said.

She moved to the umbrella table, reached into a straw beachbag and brought out a pack of cigarettes. Tina's eyes remained on the bag, lying on its side, open now. She looked at Karen lighting the cigarette, Karen sitting down in one of the deck chairs. Tina's eyes returned to the straw bag.

She said, "Is that a gun in there? In the bag?"

Karen nodded.

"Can I ask why you have it?"

"Why does anyone have a gun?" Karen said.

"I mean, of course for protection; but do you feel for some reason your life might be in danger?"

"I'm Karen Hill, I was born in Detroit, Grosse Pointe. I'm forty-four. I was married to Frank DiCilia five and a half years. I never asked him what he did. I never asked him why he had a gun. That particular gun, as a matter of fact." Karen paused. "But now I know."

"Would you tell me?"

Karen drew on the cigarette, the smoke dissolving in the afternoon glare. Karen seemed unaffected by the heat, though she was perspiring beneath the caftan, and when the writer left she'd go in the pool . . . come out, shower, it would be time for cocktails. Wait for someone to come.

She said, "Until Ed Grossi's death, I hadn't had a cigarette in sixteen years."

Tina waited. "You feel the need?"

"It's something to do."

"Are you . . . in good health?"

"Why do you ask?"

"I don't know, I just wondered. You seem a little tired."

"Or bored," Karen said. "In a way, bored. In another way—well, that's something else."

"What is?"

"Why don't you ask what my hobbies are?"

"What're your hobbies?"

"I don't have any."

"Well, what do you do all day?"

"Nothing."

'You have friends—"

"Are you asking?"

"Yeah, don't you have friends?"

Karen drew on the cigarette, looked at it and let it drop to the brick surface.

"Not really."

"Well, why don't you go out more, do things? Travel maybe."

"There are reasons," Karen said.

"What reasons?"

"I told you you weren't going to get much of a story. I don't know why you insisted."

"Because something's going on," Tina said, "and I think if you had just a little more confidence in me you might tell what it is."

"It has nothing to do with confidence."

"All right, trust. I promise I won't write anything you don't want revealed."

"Revealed," Karen said. "That's exactly the kind of word I don't want to see. Karen DiCilia's Secret Revealed."

"I don't know why I used it," Tina said, sitting forward in her chair, feeling close to something and forgetting her casual-reporter pose. "It's a written word, but it's really not the kind I use. I'm interested in your point of view, how you feel about things, rather than your effect on me. If you know what I mean."

"Which is what? How do you see me?"

"Well, I'm not sure. I mean I haven't made any judgments. Right away I think of those words again. Karen DiCilia's Secret *Not* Revealed. A very smashing looking woman who keeps to herself, has a gun—"

"Don't mention that."

"Isn't exactly hiding but seems watchful, guarded, quietly aware of something going on she won't talk about. You must realize you've got everybody wondering about you."

Karen didn't say anything. She sat with her legs crossed, one slender hand touching the side of her sunglasses.

"All right, if I do a Karen Hill rather than a Karen DiCilia," Tina said, "do you have any early pictures of yourself?"

"I may have," Karen said. "I'd have to look."

A woman by the name of Epifania Cruz, forty-two, had given her daughter and son-in-law a wooden chair that was over two hundred years old and originally from Andalucia. The chair and baby Alicia, her daughter, were brought to Miami from Cuba the night of April 27, 1961, following the defeat at the Bay of Pigs.

It was a low straight chair, more like a three-legged stool with a back support. Epifania gave it to Alicia and her son-in-law with apprehension because he was one of those who dressed like a disco dancer and spent his time at the Centro Español even though he never had a job. Epifania was in Abbey Hospital because of a problem with her colon, when she learned Alicia and her son-in-law, the pimp, had moved away quickly, getting out before they were taken to court, and had left much of what they owned in their rented home on Monegro Avenue.

Nearly a month had passed; but maybe the chair was still in the house. Epifania was told no one else had moved into it. Maybe she'd be lucky.

She went there at night. If she found the chair and carried it away, she didn't want people to see her even though she considered the chair her own property. She brought with her a large kitchen knife to use to pry open the door, but found she didn't have to. The door was unlocked.

With the street light shining in the window, Epifania could see well enough. The chair wasn't in the living room. It wasn't in the kitchen. She opened the door to the bedroom and stood in the opening. It was too dark back there to see anything. She raised her hand holding the kitchen knife, reaching for the light switch. There was an explosion and Epifania was blown back into the hall, almost to the kitchen.

Roland came out of the bedroom with the 12-gauge pump-action shotgun under his arm, reached into the kitchen to turn on the light and looked down at the woman.

He said, "Shit. You ain't Vivian."

23.

Maguire said to Lesley, "Just tell him I'm whacked out, probably coming down with something."

"I don't wonder," Lesley said. "The three of you get it on at one time, or you and the guy take turns? Hey, is he Andre?"

"Yeah, it's Andre," Maguire said, "and his wife. We haven't seen each other in awhile, so I want to take the day off, spend some time with 'em."

"He just loaned you his car a week ago, didn't he?"

"Hey, Lesley," Maguire said, "you're gonna be late for work. Tell him, okay?"

"Brad's pissed at you anyway for not coming back yesterday. He's gonna want to know where you went."

Maguire reached the end right there. He said, "Tell him whatever you want. I don't give a shit."

"Ca-al!"

She never called him Cal. Did she? What difference did it make? He went into his apartment, leaving Lesley standing by her yellow Honda. (The Mercedes was parked two blocks away.)

Jesus, hunched in front of the television set, adjusting the picture, said, "Look, the house on Monegro." A covered human form on an ambulance stretcher was being carried down the front steps as the voice-over newscaster described the mysterious shooting, the murder of a woman named Epifania Cruz. The newscaster said the police were now looking for the woman's daughter and son-in-law, the last tenants of the house.

Vivian Arzola, holding a coffeepot, watched from the stove. She said, "You know what it's like?" Neither Maguire nor Jesus looked at her, watching the woman's body being lifted into the van now. "Like in a movie, the people run out of the house, they reach safety just in time and the house blows up."

They were looking at a commercial now. When Maguire realized it he turned off the television set. Next thing they'd be watching Dinah Shore and Merv Griffin. He said, "We got to do it tonight. Figure out how and set it up—"

"If we're sure we're gonna do it," Jesus said.

They had gotten Vivian out of the house on Monegro yesterday. They weren't going to sit around here or take her from place to place. Vivian had said she wanted to get far away from here. It wasn't worth it, looking over her shoulder all the time. She had to go someplace else.

"It's *how* we do it, not *if,*" Maguire said. "It's got to be at the DiCilia house."

"Why?" Jesus said.

"Because the police were there already"—Maguire speaking quietly, wanting Jesus to relax and listen—"when Roland tried to grab your sister. Okay, he comes to try again, armed, huh? Only this time we're there. You're defending your sister, you shoot him."

"Me? I thought you were gonna shoot him."

"One or the other," Maguire said. "You know how to fire a gun, don't you?"

"Sure, I know that. But I never shot at anybody."

"Let's talk about—first, how do we get him there?" Maguire said. "He comes because he thinks Vivian's in the house."

"You're crazy you think I'm going there," Vivian said.

"You don't have to go there. I'm saying he thinks you're there because we get him to believe it. Like, say I call you from there later. I say, 'Okay, Vivian, it's all set. We'll pick you up, you spend the night here and take you to the police first thing in the morning.' You say something, he hears your voice, he knows it's you."

"I don't understand," Vivian said, then began to nod.

"Yeah, the tap on the phone. I can't even think straight."

"What if he don't?" Jesus said. "If he's busy looking for Vivian and he don't listen to it?"

"I don't know," Maguire said, wondering if he had to tell Karen about it and not wanting to. Though if they had to wait around a few days until Roland picked up the tape—it might turn out he'd have to tell her. But he didn't want to bring her into it. He wanted to get it done and present her with it. There, the guy's off your back. Making it look, not easy exactly, but not too hard either. There. You have any other problems?

He said to Jesus, "What's the guy's name working for him?"

"Lionel Oliva."

"Okay, you tell Lionel you know where Vivian is. You say you found out Vivian's gonna be there tonight. Your sister told you."

"What if he asks why I'm telling him?" Jesus said. "He knows I won't do any favor for Roland."

"Tell him—what if you tell him you're setting Roland up for somebody?"

"Then what's Lionel get out of it? He says bullshit. If he tells Roland and Roland gets taken out, who's gonna pay him?"

"You tell him you'll pay him," Maguire said. "What's it worth to him?"

"He's gonna be scared. You miss, the first one Roland go sees is Lionel, knowing he was set up."

"How about a grand?"

"You kidding? He'd do it himself for a grand."

"And get some more stitches in his head," Maguire said. "I've seen Lionel. *That* Lionel? No, we do it. But he sets it up. All he has to do, tell Roland he knows Vivian's gonna be there tonight. That's all he knows. He heard it from you and you told him not to tell anybody, acting very mysterious about it. You think he can do it?"

"Yeah, he can do that."

"And act dumb?"

"Easy," Jesus said.

"Then Roland gets the tape, hears Vivian's voice, he knows it's true. Even if he doesn't get the tape, he's got to go find out after Lionel tells him. But it's better if he does, because then he hears Vivian's voice, hears she's going to the police—it's much better that way. We don't want Lionel telling him all that and mess it up."

Jesus said, "Okay, but what gun do we use? I don't want to use mine, have to get rid of it after."

"No, we don't get rid of it," Maguire said. "That's what I've been talking about. We call the cops, we have to have a gun to show 'em, right?"

"You want to call the cops?"

Jesus, Maguire thought. He said, "Look. The guy comes in to rape your sister. You shoot him. *Some*body shoots him. You don't throw his body in the Intercoastal, you call the cops and give 'em the gun. That's what you *do*. Okay, then Vivian reads about it in the paper. Roland Crowe killed in rape attempt. Vivian goes to the police, tells 'em she knows Roland killed Ed Grossi. The police let the other guy go."

"I'm telling you, he better be dead," Vivian said, "or I don't say a word to them, not even my name."

"He'll be dead," Maguire said. He looked at Jesus. "You don't want to use your gun—okay, tell your sister there's a gun upstairs in Karen's bedroom, top dresser drawer. Tell her to sneak it out of there, bring it down to her room. We slip in the house after dark, she gives it to us. It was Frank DiCilia's gun. They want to bust somebody for possession they can dig up Frank. But bring your own anyway, just in case."

"Then what?" Jesus said. "He comes in—when do we do it?"

"That part, we'll have to wait and see," Maguire said.

Karen watched him coming out from the house. She stood at the shallow end of the pool drying herself lightly with a beach towel. He was putting on his sunglasses now, taking her all in.

"Do you really have that much nerve," Karen said, "or're you showing off?"

"What nerve?"

"Using the phone. You know he's going to hear it. You disguise your voice or what?"

"He's got to do more'n hear me, he's got to catch me."

"Who were you calling?"

"The guy I work for. Find out if I still have a job."

"Does it matter?"

"Well, I guess I'd rather quit than be fired. But I don't feel like working. He was busy, so I still don't know."

"I can't imagine you being worried about it," Karen said, "the job."

"I'm not worried, I want to know how he feels."

Karen said, "I saw the news this morning . . . the house. Strange, the woman wasn't Vivian."

"No, we got her out of there. I forgot to tell you."

"Something's going on," Karen said. "In fact I think there's quite a lot you haven't told me."

Maguire watched her walk to the table to get something out of a straw bag. The slim brown body. Effortless moves. The quiet tone. He'd bet she drove a car fast and without effort; he saw the two of them, briefly, in the white Alpha Romeo heading for southern Spain.

He said, "I've been thinking the same thing. Like you know something you're not telling."

"What's Karen DiCilia's secret," Karen said. "Read the latest speculation in next month's *Goldcoaster*. Though this one's going to be on Karen Hill."

"Who's she?" Maguire said.

"Who knows," Karen said.

"You going out tonight?"

"Like where?"

He wanted to say to her, It won't be long; hang on. But said, "I'll see you later then, okay?"

"Fine. Anytime."

He left Karen in her backyard world putting on sunglasses, lighting a cigarette. Maguire walked up S.E. Seventeenth toward the beach, where he'd left the Mercedes. He wondered if she did know something she wasn't telling. He wondered about the photos of her in the locked room. When this was over he'd ask her about them.

Was she lighting a cigarette when he left?

He wondered when she had started smoking. Maybe he hadn't been paying attention lately, looking but overlooking, missing something.

Karen had a glass of distilled water from the refrigerator. She left Marta in the kitchen cleaning vegetables for dinner. Moving along the back hall, Karen paused, looked around, stepped into Marta's room and quietly closed the door. The cassette recorder was still beneath the bed, with a box of cassette cartridges. Karen brought them out, hunching down on her elbows and knees. She changed the setting from "Record" to "Rewind," stopped it, pushed the "Play" button and within a few moments heard Maguire's voice.

"Vivian? Hi, it's all set. We'll pick you up at eleven-thirty and bring you right here. Then first thing in the morning we go to Miami."

Vivian's voice said, "I'm so afraid he's going to find me. I can't eat, I can't sleep. God, I can't *think.*"

Maguire's voice said, "Tomorrow it'll be over. The Miami Police'll pick him up, you identify him, that's it."

Vivian's voice said, "I'll be so glad when it's over."

Maguire's voice said, "Eleven-thirty, Vivian. See you then."

Karen played the tape back and listened to it again, twice.

She was surprised, puzzled.

Then annoyed.

Karen ejected the tape cartridge. Holding it in her hand, she got a blank cartridge from the box, snapped the new one in position and pushed the recorder and the box back under Marta's bed.

24.

Karen bathed and dressed. She had a martini in the living room while she watched the news. At a quarter to seven she went into the kitchen carrying a handbag and the keys to Frank's Seville, in the garage.

Marta looked at her, surprised. "I was going to ask if you're ready for dinner."

"I'm sorry, I thought I told you," Karen said, "I'm having dinner out." She looked at the salad greens drying on the counter. "You haven't started anything yet, have you?"

"No—" She seemed to want to say more.

"What's the matter?"

"I don't want to be alone," Marta said, "if Roland comes."

"I thought your brother picks up the tape."

"Remember, I tole you he doesn't do it anymore."

"Well, it's up to you," Karen said. "But if you don't want to open the door when he comes, then don't."

"That wouldn't stop him."

"Maybe not. It seems funny, though, to be offering you advice," Karen said. "I tried to help you before. You had a chance to have him arrested and you didn't."

"Of course. For the same reason I don't want to be alone with him. I'm scared, I don't know what to do."

"And I don't know what to tell you," Karen said. "You're afraid to let him in and you're afraid not to."

"I wish things would be the same, the way it used to be," Marta said.

"Wouldn't it be nice," Karen said. "So, are you going to give him the tape?"

"I guess so."

Karen jiggled her keys, getting the one for the Seville ready. She said, "Well, I have to go," but remained by the kitchen table, looking at Marta. "I think what I would do, I'd leave the tape for him outside the door and get away from here for awhile. Maybe a few days. You know? Instead of putting yourself in the middle of something that really doesn't concern you."

"Leave here?"

"Why not? What's anyone done for you lately?"

Just in time.

Roland wheeled his Coupe de Ville into the drive as Marta was backing out, saw her brakelights flash and, before she knew it, was pressed against her rear bumper.

Out of the car Roland said, "Hey, don't leave on my account. Where we going?" He looked toward the open garage doors and at the house, up at the second-floor windows, as though he might catch someone watching him.

Roland picked up the envelope with his name on it —ROLAND, in big blue letters—from the steps and moved aside to let Marta unlock the door.

"There's nobody home," she said.

"Don't look like it," Roland said. "I ain't gonna play house with you today, sugar, I want to use your telephone." He dialed the one in the kitchen, waited, said, "Son of a bitch," and hung up. "Where's Karen at?"

"She went out to dinner."

"Who with?"

"Nobody. Alone."

" 'Less she's meeting him, huh? Let's go in your bedroom and listen to this one," Roland said, holding up the envelope. "Many calls today?"

"Only a few," Marta said.

Minutes later, in Marta's room, after playing the tape and hearing nothing, Roland said, "I'd say that's less than a few. Or else this here's the wrong one."

"I took it out of the machine," Marta said.

"And I know you wouldn't lie to me," Roland said, straightening up from the recorder on the chair, standing close to Marta, the bed behind her. "Would you?"

"I have no reason to lie," she said.

"You got a nice body, you know it?"

Marta stood rigid, her head turned away from his chest.

"But I don't have time just now to make you happy. Your tough luck," Roland said, going into the kitchen. He picked up the wall phone and dialed again.

This time he said, "You dink, where you been?"

Lionel's voice said, "I was in the toilet a minute."

"Drinking beer—how many you have?"

"I'm sitting here, I have to do something," Lionel's voice said, the sound of a salsa beat behind him.

"Hang on a sec." Roland looked at Marta. "Go on out in the living room." He waited until she was in the hall before saying to Lionel, "Get in your boat and bring it up to Bahía Mar."

Lionel's voice said, "Man, it's gonna be dark soon."

"I hope so," Roland said. "I'll meet you there by the gas pumps in about a hour." He started to hang up, then said, "Hey, Jesus say his sister told him or what?"

"No, he didn't say anything about his sister," Lionel's voice said. "He say it was Vivian."

Roland held the phone away from him, away from the Caribbean jukebox music behind Lionel. Sure as hell—the sound of a car starting up outside, revving up, then banging something and a terrible sound of metal scraping metal.

"Shit," Roland said. "You be there." He banged the phone into its cradle and ran out of the kitchen to the side door.

Marta had her car turned around on the lawn; she cut across the drive and was screeching away, leaving the front left fender of Roland's Coupe de Ville all torn to hell.

The Palm Bay waiter said to Karen, "The gentleman at the bar would like to join you for a drink, if he may."

Karen looked from the booth she was in to a man with gray-styled hair and a paisley jacket. Half-turned from the bar he raised his drink to her.

"Does he know my name?" Karen said.

"Oh, yes. He said, 'Ask Mrs. DiCilia.' "

"Tell him he's mistaken," Karen said.

The waiter smiled. "You don't want a drink with him?"

"I said tell him he's mistaken."

"Very good," the waiter said.

When the man with the gray-styled hair came over, Karen said, "I don't know you. I don't intend to. Would you go away, please?"

"If you're alone, no harm in having a drink, a nice chat—"

"Beat it," Karen said. She stared up at him until he mumbled, "Sorry," and went back to the bar.

See? Nothing to it.

The look was important. Icy calm, unwavering; the tone quiet, somewhat bored. Maybe a little more work on the tone, keeping the voice low.

Maybe another one would come along. The rescuers—

The Maguires.

Maguire was going to stick his neck out all the way, showing off, and never be heard of again. The natural-born loser. She could try to prevent it, within reason; but if he insisted on playing the rescuer, then she'd have to let him. Karen Hill DiCilia was at the Palm Bay Club the night it happened. Or she was home, but it wasn't exactly clear what had happened, Karen Hill's part in it. Karen Hill seemed cooperative. Yes, she knew the deceased, was acquainted with him. But Karen Hill obviously knew more than she was telling.

The waiter came over and said, "If I may disturb you, please. The gentleman at the table by the window—"

Karen looked over. "Does he know my name?"

Marta drove all the way to Jesus' apartment on Alhambra, Coral Gables, and got in after she proved to the manager she was Jesus' sister and not some girl who wanted to rip him off. God, all the things there were to go through and worry about—walking back and forth in Jesus' living room, walking to the kitchen, walking to the front window, looking out at the street and the cars going by, some with their lights on already, the time passing so fast, rushing her and not giving her a chance to think. She got the phone number from her purse, the Casa Loma, and dialed, then had to wait as the phone rang at least twenty times. When the woman answered, Marta asked if she could please speak to her brother, the man visiting Mr. Maguire. Marta could hear sounds of voices talking and an audience laughing, applauding on the phone, having a good time, as she waited again.

When Jesus was on the phone she said, "I left there. I'm not going back."

"Where are you?"

"I'm at your place, but I'm leaving here, too."

"Did Roland come?"

"Did he come—he was gonna take my clothes off again and I ran out. I'm not going back."

"Calm yourself," Jesus said. "I can't hear you very well, this TV playing."

"I'm not going back there," Marta said.

"You have to be in the house," Jesus said. "You understand you have to be there."

"What is it to me," Marta said, "or you? It's none of our business. What do we get out of it?"

"Listen, stay there," Jesus said. "I'll come soon as I can, and we'll talk about it. All right?"

"I'm gonna have to go get her," Jesus said to Maguire.

"Did he pick up the tape?"

"Yeah, but he tried something, so she ran out and went to my place. She'll be all right."

"You sure?"

"If I take Vivian's car"—looking at Vivian on the bed with the newspaper on her lap, watching them—"I can go get Marta, talk to her first. See, then bring her to the house and meet you there. Take maybe an hour, a little more."

"Did she put the gun in her room?"

"I didn't ask her, but I know she did."

Maguire didn't like it. He said, "Call Marta back. Have her come here."

"She won't. I have to talk to her first. Then everything be all right."

"You can't drive up to the house in Vivian's car."

"No, we leave it at my place, take Marta's. Roland comes, sees Marta's car, he thinks oh, she's back. Good."

Maguire said to Vivian, "Is it okay with you?"

"What do I have to say about it? Nothing," Vivian said. "All I want to know is he's dead."

"All right," Maguire said to Jesus. "But you got to get back by nine-thirty quarter to ten, the latest."

"Easy," Jesus said. "Don't worry."

25.

Maguire's plan was coming apart.

An hour ago it had seemed close to foolproof. Drop in on Karen, sit around till about ten. Say he was tired or didn't feel good and leave. Park up by the beach and walk back. Marta lets him in the side door. He and Jesus wait in Marta's room for Roland to come. Let him enter the house. Say hi, how you doing? Marta screams (optional). Hit him.

But Marta was in Coral Gables, and Jesus had to talk to her and get her back.

And Karen wasn't home. The house was dark, the three-car garage empty.

He could say to himself, No, it's going to work. Don't worry. Keep your eyes open. You see it's not going to work or too chancy, bail out. You don't *have* to be here.

But reassurances didn't relieve the bad feeling, the doubt beginning to nag him.

Maguire drove the Mercedes into the garage, closed the door from the outside and walked around the house, past the empty patio to the French doors.

There was some definition to the shapes in the darkness: the hedges, the pool, the umbrella table, the yard misty in a pale wash of moonlight. There were specks of moving light on the Intercoastal, the deep darkness beyond the yard. There was the sound of crickets. And now Gretchen barking, inside the house. There was no reason to be as quiet as he might be. Maguire pulled the sleeve of his jacket down over his hand, held it in his fist, punched through the pane of glass next to the door latch and he was inside, Gretchen running up to him, barking.

Moving through the sitting room, his hand feeling the crown of the Louis XVI chair, he told Gretchen to be nice and wondered: If Karen knew she was coming home after dark, why didn't she leave a light on?

Because Marta must've still been home.

Then why didn't Marta tell them Karen had gone out? If she did, why didn't Jesus mention it?

Because they had no practice in this kind of thing, that's why, Maguire thought. And you better get your ass out of here.

But he moved from the front hall to the back hall to Marta's room, pulled down the shades and turned on a lamp. Okay, Jesus had said yes, he *knew* Marta had gotten the gun from upstairs. But where would she hide it.

Roland said to Lionel, "Look, I ain't gonna argue with you. Go on get drunk, sleep on the beach, I don't give a shit where, and pick up the boat in the morning. Now hand the suitcase here and push me off, goddamn it." Man, to get through to some people.

The eighteen-footer rumbled away from the dock behind the thin beam of its spotlight, passing the fantails of the motorcruisers and sailers tied up in their slips, heading out into the channel now, Roland keeping the revs low, bearing to starboard as he pictured the map of the Intercoastal, this little section of it. Finding his way through canals and watercourses, natural or manmade, wasn't anything new. Across the Harborage and where it opened up at the river—hearing a cruiser honking at the drawbridge down there—head for the second point of land and the house sitting there. He figured about a five-minute ride. There were support stanchions along the seawall; he'd tie up to one of them. In the meantime—wedging a hip against the wheel and zipping open the canvas suitcase—he'd get his twelve-gauge put together.

It took Maguire nearly ten minutes of looking through every drawer, the closet, and the bed to convince himself the gun, the one Jesus *knew* was in the room, wasn't.

Andre Patterson would look at him and shake his head, Man, the people you associate with. Say to Andre, But look. What do they have to do? Practically nothing. Andre would say, That's exactly what they doing. Nothing. Where they at?

They'll be here.

In the meantime, run upstairs and get the gun. Before Karen comes home. Wherever Karen went.

Maguire turned off the lamp, felt his way out to the front hall and moved up the stairway. Gretchen had gone off somewhere.

When Roland saw the house dark it made him wonder for a moment. How come? Then accepted it as he crossed the yard toward the house. They went to get Vivian, that's why. Both of them.

But at the French doors, about to put the rubber-padded butt of the shotgun through the glass, seeing it busted already, he said, No, they didn't.

Somebody was home, and he bet he knew who it was, too. Somebody besides little Gretchen panting, trying to climb his leg. Roland sat down in the Louis XVI chair to pull off his cowboy boots, whispering, "You like to smell my feet, do you, huh? Come on up here you little thing. I don't like to do this, Gretchie, no I don't, but I got to." He put his hand over Gretchen's muzzle, clamping it over her nose and mouth and held the squirming furry body until it shuddered and became limp.

Roland went through the hall to the living room, looked in, came back past the stairway and paused. Was that a sound up there? Like a drawer being shut? Roland went through the back hall to Marta's room—no Cubans hiding under the bed—came out and turned into the kitchen. There was a soft orange glow on the telephone to show where it hung on the wall. Roland got an idea. He'd memorized Frank DiCilia's private number once. Now, if he could remember it—

Maguire closed the top drawer. He opened, looked through and closed every drawer in the dresser. He looked in the drawers of the two nightstand tables. He looked under the pillows and the mattress. Shit. Andre Patterson would say, Get your ass out, boy.

No, be cool. Where would she put it?

He went back to the dresser and got the key to the next room out of the drawer. It was possible—she'd decided to put the gun back with Frank's stuff, his papers, his money. Maguire unlocked the door and went in. No light showed in the window; the draperies were closed. He turned on the desk lamp. Straightening then, his eyes went to the photographs on the wall, the shots of Karen.

The telephone rang.

Maguire jumped and Andre Patterson, watching, would say, See?

The telephone rang.

Maguire went over to it sitting on the desk and looked at the number in the center of the dial. Not Karen's number, a private line.

The telephone rang.

He'd wait for it to stop. And then thought, What if it's Karen? If she knew, somehow, he was in the house—

The telephone rang.

—Didn't want him to answer on her phone and have it recorded, so—no, both lines would be tapped. That wasn't it.

The telephone rang.

But it still could be Karen. Or Marta. It could be anybody. It could be Marta with Jesus, knowing he'd be looking for the gun. No—why this phone?

The telephone rang.

It would stop.

The telephone rang.

The telephone rang.

Shit, Maguire said and picked it up.

"How you doing?" Roland's voice said. "You coming down or you want me to come up?"

"So this parrot went to take a piss, see, and drowned in the toilet. How you doing?" Roland said, coming out of the dark bedroom into lamplight, the pump-action shotgun leading.

"In the commode was the word," Maguire said, sitting in the swivel chair behind the desk, trying to look calm. Where the hell else was there to go?

"I think it sounds better toilet. Where's Vivian at?"

"I don't know any Vivian. Vivian who?"

"Shit," Roland said, "we gonna have a question-answer period or we gonna get to it?"

"I got nothing to tell you," Maguire said.

"Then you might as well be dead, huh?" Roland put the shotgun on him.

"Unless you want to try a few questions and see where they lead," Maguire said.

"I got one," Roland said, "only one. Where's Vivian?"

"I can't do it like that, have it on my conscience."

"How can you do it?"

"I don't see a way yet."

"Then die looking, you dumb shit. It's up to you."

"You want to go for two counts, is that it?"

"Two?" Roland said. "If I notched my gunbutt you'd get splinters running your hand on it, you dink. I don't care about numbers. You're just another one."

"But it's money what it's all about. Right?"

"What do you make, two bucks an hour? Want to give me about a hunnert?"

"I don't have it, no. But I know where I could get some." Maguire looked up at the photos on the wall.

Roland glanced over and back to Maguire, then turned to look at the display of photos again.

"What's this all about, you know? Puts up pitchers of herself." Roland stepped closer. "And somebody else there, huh? I thought they was all her when I first seen 'em."

"I think she comes up here and plays pretend," Maguire said. "Get her mind off things."

"Pretend what?"

"The mystery lady, I think. Like that other one."

"Who's she?"

"I forgot her name." Maguire heard the car then.

Roland heard it, too. He came around with the shotgun. "She bringing Vivian?"

"Or cops. You gonna wait and see?"

"Stay put," Roland said. He stepped into the bedroom.

Maguire heard a door, downstairs, open and close. He couldn't see Roland now. But heard his voice from the upstairs hall. "Come on up, join the party."

He could go out the window—if it opened and there was no screen to fool with. He didn't owe Karen anything. It was the other way around, all the time he'd put in. She owed him more than she'd ever know.

But he remained in the swivel chair. Probably wouldn't make it out the window anyway—Roland moved for a big man. So what could he do? Nothing. The hell with Andre Patterson there watching, shaking his head.

Karen was coming in, seeing him at the desk. Christ, Karen shaking her head, too. Roland came in behind her saying, "I hope we can get this cleared up, what's going on."

Karen took a cigarette out of a pack in her straw handbag and laid the bag on the desk.

"You have a light?"

"I used to chew, but I never smoked," Roland said. "It's bad for you."

Karen took a lighter from the bag and snapped it several times. "I went to Miami for dinner. Alone." She dropped the lighter on the desk and raised her hip to sit against the corner, picking up the handbag and resting it on her lap now as she felt inside.

"You got a match?" Roland said to Maguire.

"I don't smoke."

"That's smart," Roland said. He looked at Karen. "I believe you. It's this dink here causing all the commotion. See, he was gonna bring Vivian here—the way I figure it—and try and get a lot of money out of you to help her get away." He stopped. "You know why?"

Karen looked up from the handbag on her lap, pausing. "Yes, I know."

"Then they did talk to you."

"Not really. I found out on my own."

Maguire kept looking at her as Roland said, "Don't believe everything you hear, it ain't required. So he comes to the house wants to talk to you, see if he can bring Vivian, and you're not home. So what does he do, he busts in."

"Why?" Karen said.

"To wait for you."

"Unh-unh, to wait for *you,"* Karen said. "That was the whole idea."

"Wait for *me?* Why would he do that?"

Jesus Christ, Maguire thought.

"To kill you," Karen said.

"Shit, he don't even have a gun."

"I do," Karen said.

Her hand came out of the straw bag gripping the Beretta and fired it point blank at Roland's bright-blue suitjacket and fired it again and fired it again and fired it again, until Roland stumbled against the file cabinet and went down on top of his shotgun, tried then as if to do a pushup and fell heavily and didn't move again.

Karen stood up, watching Roland. After a moment she laid the gun on the desk. She said to Maguire, who was staring at her, "How did you get in?"

"I broke in. The glass door in the sitting room."

"No, that's how he broke in," Karen said. "You weren't here."

"Look, I'll tell what happened, or anything you want. I'm not worried about being involved."

"You weren't here," Karen said again. "So you'd better leave, okay? I have to call the police."

"Wait a minute," Maguire said, getting up. "This was my idea, right? The whole thing."

"It wasn't a very good one," Karen said. "What did you expect to get out of it?"

Maguire was confused now, frowning. Was she kidding? She couldn't be. "What'd we talk about all the time? Getting him off your back, going away, traveling together."

Karen picked up the lighter, flicked it once, and lit her cigarette. Looking at him she said, "Did I promise you anything?"

"It's all we talked about."

"We did?"

"Jesus Christ, I paid Jesus five grand—"

"Of my money. Don't you think I checked it? With you two in the house."

"Jesus Christ," Maguire said. He couldn't believe it. "*Us* two—I paid Lionel a grand out of my own money."

"And I believe I saved your life," Karen said. "But I'll pay you whatever you spent out of pocket." She walked to the file cabinet, stepping over Roland, and opened it.

Maguire watched her. He said, "You didn't want to get out of this at all, did you? You get some kind of a kick out of it, playing a role. Like the dolphins—they're putting up with all that shit, you turn 'em loose. What do they do? They come back to the phony world to play games. You're just like the fucking dolphins, you know it?"

"Here's your thousand," Karen said.

"You'll get your picture in the paper again, act mysterious—you gonna have room to put it up?"

"I enjoyed meeting you," Karen said. "Now beat it. Okay?"

ABOUT THE AUTHOR

ELMORE LEONARD has written over fifteen novels and numerous short stories, several of which have been turned into successful films including *3:10 to Yuma* and *Valdez Is Coming.* He has also written the screenplays for such films as *Joe Kidd,* starring Clint Eastwood, and *Mr. Majestyk,* starring Charles Bronson. His novel, *Hombre,* was chosen as one of the twenty-five best Western novels ever written by the Western Writers of America and *The Switch,* published by Bantam, was nominated by the Mystery Writers of America for the Edgar Allan Poe Award for the best paperback of 1978.